HER ONLY WISH

A SEASON IN PINECRAFT, BOOK 2

HER ONLY WISH

SHELLEY SHEPARD GRAY

THORNDIKE PRESS
A part of Gale, a Cengage Company

Copyright © 2023 by Shelley Shepard Gray.
Thorndike Press, a part of Gale, a Cengage Company.

Thorndike Press® Large Print Christian Fiction.
The text of this Large Print edition is unabridged.
Other aspects of the book may vary from the original edition.
Set in 16 pt. Plantin.

LIBRARY OF CONGRESS CIP DATA ON FILE.
CATALOGUING IN PUBLICATION FOR THIS BOOK
IS AVAILABLE FROM THE LIBRARY OF CONGRESS.

ISBN-13: 979-8-88578-870-0 (hardcover alk. paper).

Published in 2023 by arrangement with Revell Books, a division of Baker Publishing Group.

Printed in Mexico
Print Number: 1   Print Year: 2023

Having hope will give you courage.

Job 11:18

If your mind can conceive it and your heart can believe it, you can achieve it.

Amish saying

1

June

It was a beautiful morning in Pinecraft, Florida. Once again, the sun was out, the flowers were blooming, and there was a slight undercurrent of salt in the air. It was the kind of morning that made one want to look up into the cloudless sky and give thanks for the chance to experience such beauty.

That's why it was a real shame that Mary Margaret Raber was beginning to get on Betsy's nerves.

No, that wasn't exactly true. Mary had been grating on her nerves for a good fifteen minutes. It was only in the last two or three minutes that Betsy had decided she'd had enough. There was only so much unsolicited advice a girl wanted to get before drinking two cups of coffee.

"Do you hear what I'm saying, Betsy?" Mary asked.

Taking note of the spotless kitchen, Betsy pasted on a fake smile. "Jah. I've been hearing your words loud and clear."

"Whew. For a moment there, you were looking so confused I thought maybe I was giving you too much advice." Mary brushed a strand of blond hair from her cheek. "Jayson's told me that sometimes I have a tendency to go on and on."

"Don't worry. You were fine." She just wasn't going to take any of her friend's advice.

Relief entered Mary's light brown eyes. "Oh? Well, that's gut. Wonderful-gut."

Betsy smiled as she tapped her foot. Her friend needed to wrap this lecture up real soon or else Betsy was going to do it for her. Not that anyone would blame her.

The simple truth was that even though Mary had been married barely a year, she was already acting as if she had all the answers. She'd also been acting a bit full of herself . . . like she knew best.

About everything.

If Betsy didn't love her so much, she'd tell her girlfriend that this absolutely wasn't the case.

However, since Mary and Jayson had invited her to stay in their guest room for a whole month, Betsy did what she usually did. She smiled, looked grateful, and mentally planned to do what she wanted anyway.

When at last Mary took a breath, she studied Betsy closely. "You sure are quiet. Do you understand what I'm trying to tell you?"

"I do." Leaning against the kitchen counter, she crossed her arms over her chest. "Perfectly."

For the first time in the past hour, Mary looked wary. "Betsy, all I'm trying to say is that you only got here two days ago. I'm sure you're tired. Don't you think you need more rest?"

"I do not. Now that we've had our chat, I'm going to head over to Snow Bird Golf Course and ask them about taking golf lessons."

Mary frowned. "Oh, all right. Well, yes. I guess I could rearrange my day. We should go soon, since it's so warm out."

Mary was four months pregnant. She was still nauseous from time to time, always ready for a nap, and usually wanted to talk about her amazing husband Jayson, Jayson's wonderful-gut job, her pregnancy, or all things baby. Betsy didn't blame her one bit. If their positions were reversed, she'd probably feel the same way.

Perhaps they should have a talk after all.

"May we go sit down for a minute?"

"Of course. Where would you like to sit? On the lanai?" Mary's voice was hopeful.

Their covered screen porch was lovely. "That's perfect. I'll go get me another cup of coffee and you a glass of lemonade."

"Oh, you're the guest. I can get them."

"Mary Margaret, I'm going to be here for a month. I don't want you to wait on me."

As Mary walked off to go put her feet up, Betsy went to the kitchen, got more coffee, poured a glass of lemonade, and then joined Mary on the lanai.

The area was big enough to hold a table, four chairs, two cushioned lounge chairs, and a small love seat. Everything was done in greens and teal colors. There were festive, bright-colored pillows on everything, an outside carpet, and about five terracotta pots filled with blooming flowers.

"I know I've told you before, but this is my favorite spot in your house. It's so pretty out here," she said as she sat down.

"It's mine too. Jayson built the addition himself a few months after we got married."

"He did a nice job."

"I think the baby is going to like being out here too."

"I'm sure she will."

Mary chuckled. "You're as certain about

10

me having a girl as Jayson is about having a boy."

"I can't help myself. I'm sure you're going to be rocking a sweet miniature version of yourself in here before you know it."

"Whatever the Lord wants is fine with me."

"I understand." Taking a fortifying sip of coffee, Betsy knew she couldn't delay the inevitable any longer. "I think we need to talk."

"I know. You don't want me trying to mother you, do you?"

Betsy stilled. "You knew what I was going to say?"

"We're good enough friends for me to know what your expression looks like when you've reached the end of your patience. You don't want to rest another two days, do you?"

She shook her head. "I not only don't want to do that, I'm not going to." Looking at Mary intently, she added, "I'm grateful to you and Jayson for your hospitality, but I tried to be upfront about what I wanted to do during my visit. I even told you that I didn't mind going to a motel."

"You staying in a motel by yourself was a terrible idea."

Betsy smiled at her. "It probably was. I

am glad I'm here instead of a motel — but as much as I like you, I'm not going to give up my list."

"Your bucket list."

"It's not a bucket list. A bucket list is a list of things to do before you die. I have a list of things to do to make me feel like I'm finally living. It's my life list."

Because Mary still looked skeptical, Betsy kept talking. "Don't you understand? All my life I've been standing on the sidelines, watching everyone else try new things. I don't want to wait any longer."

"But your lungs . . . Betsy, you know your mother sent me a letter with all your medical history and doctor contact information."

"And you might recall that I was so mad at her for doing that, I barely talked to her for a week."

"She wants you to be safe."

"She wants me to be five years old again. Don't you think it would be strange if I didn't already have all that information? I'm twenty-three years old. Of course I have it!"

Mary flushed. "I . . . I should've realized that."

"I need you to stop acting like I can't tell when I need to use my inhaler or take breaks or call the doctor."

"You're right." She reached out and

clasped Betsy's hand. "I'm so sorry. I'll be better."

"It's okay if you don't want to hold your tongue or you don't feel comfortable letting me do things. But if that's how it is, then let me stay someplace else. We'll still be able to see each other, you know."

"I want you here. I'll stop hovering. I promise."

"I'm going to hold you to that."

"You should." Looking sheepish, Mary added, "Jayson even told me last night that I was sounding too much like a mother hen."

Betsy smiled. "I knew I liked him."

Thirty minutes later, Betsy was walking down Bahia Vista Street toward Snow Bird Golf Course. Soon after their talk, Mary had lain down to take a nap. Betsy hoped she hadn't hurt her friend's feelings but was pleased with herself for initiating such an honest conversation. She'd gone through far too much to put her list aside.

The reminder of the many hospital visits and tests she'd had to endure made some of her happy mood fade. Those episodes had been painful and frightening. They'd also been exhausting, because she'd gotten into an unfortunate routine of worrying about her mother's feelings more than her own. She adored her parents and her brother, but for once she didn't want to do everything they suggested just to make them happy.

She'd given them an ultimatum a month ago — saying that she needed to be gone for a whole month and that they needed to accept that fact. Or prepare themselves for her to move out permanently.

Pushing the dark thoughts away, she scanned the busy streets, looking for the golf course's sign.

And there it was. Snow Bird Golf Course, written in plain block letters in blue against a shiny black background. It was attractive and somehow looked very Plain at the same time.

She turned down the narrow lane. And gasped. There, in front of her, was a hidden gem. A bright green golf course with yellow flags at each hole, wide limestone gravel paths, bright white golf carts, a driving range, a putting green, and finally, the cutest little pale blue building with shiny black trim.

Picking up her pace, she walked toward the building, stepping off the limestone path and onto the soft green grass. Pleased with herself for not taking the meandering route, she looked around and smiled when she saw a tiny brown bunny.

"Aren't you cute?" she murmured. "Are there bunnies like you all over this place?"

The rabbit froze, then hopped away, vanishing in seconds. Figuring rabbits were rabbits, whether they lived in Kentucky or Florida, Betsy chuckled, then kept walking, scanning the vicinity as she went. There were hydrangea bushes, lovely flowering bougainvillea, and a small pond off to her right. Anxious to take it all in, she slowed her pace.

"Hey!"

She kept walking.

"Hey! Amish lady in the orange dress! Stop!"

She looked down at herself, realized the voice was calling out to her, and stopped — about three feet from where a golf ball flew across the green. If she hadn't stopped, it would've hit her.

A golf cart zipped forward and stopped next to her. One of the two men in the cart got out.

By his dress, he was obviously Amish too. Straw hat, short-sleeved shirt, long pants. He also had blond hair so bleached it looked white, gray eyes, and a really great tan.

"Hey, are you all right?" he asked.

"Jah. I d-don't know what h-happened." Hating that her stutter had returned, Betsy tried to calm herself. "D-do people really have to worry about d-dodging golf balls all the time?"

"They do when they're walking in the middle of the fairway," the other guy in the golf cart said. "What were you thinking?"

Stung by his rude tone, she propped one hand on her hip. "I was thinking that I needed to get to that b-building right there."

"Why didn't you stay on the cart path?"

"I . . . I didn't know I had to."

"Really?"

The man's voice was so filled with sarcasm, it took the edge off her nervousness. "S-sorry, but you show me a sign that says stay off the grass and I'll do it. Otherwise, I think you need to mind your own business."

The man in the cart scowled at her. "I'm going ahead, August."

The man who had gotten off the cart — August, she supposed — looked like he was trying not to laugh. "Jah. You do that. I'm gonna help this lady here."

"You want me to wait for you?"

"Better not. There's a foursome two holes behind us."

When the cart drove off, August turned to

her. "Come on," he said as he reached for her elbow. "We need to get back on the cart path so we don't get dinged."

Betsy hurried to the path but started to feel like she'd just made a complete fool of herself. "I'm guessing there aren't any signs because everyone knows not to walk on the grass?"

"I'm afraid so. But, um, I agree that a sign or two might be a good idea."

"You know, you really don't need to walk me to the building."

"I think I do."

"No you don't. I was looking for the person who runs the golf course." She smiled, hoping she sounded far more confident than she felt. "I-I promise, I won't veer off the sidewalk again." She didn't want to offend him, but she wasn't there to be escorted like an errant child.

August looked bemused. "Actually, I was going there myself."

"Because?"

"Because I'm the manager of the course."

They stopped in front of the sign mounted to the siding of the building. He pointed to the discreetly written words under Snow Bird Golf Course. August Troyer, Manager.

And then it hit her. "You're August."

"I am. I'm August Troyer, the manager of

the golf course. I'm the guy you came to see." His grin broadened. "What luck, huh?"

"Jah," she muttered as she followed him inside. It looked like they both had some explaining to do.

August Troyer was handsome, personable, and very full of himself. And now he realized she didn't even know enough about golf to stay on the cart paths.

How in the world was she going to get up the nerve to ask him about golf lessons?

All of the sudden, her grand plan of completing the things on her life list was starting to feel very overwhelming.

Pretty much impossible.

2

His buddy Nate was going to tease him about cutting out in the middle of a round for years to come, but August didn't care. All he cared about was that this pretty young thing, so prim and proper looking on the outside but so spunky on the inside, had somehow crossed his path. He wasn't going to ignore her.

As far as August was concerned, the Lord had decided that it was the perfect day for them to meet each other — how else could one explain such a chance meeting?

He walked over to the counter that ran the length of the small pro shop and turned to face her. "How may I help you?"

"Well . . ."

"August?" Uncle Gideon called out. "Whatcha doing here? I thought you were going to play a round with Nate."

"I was, but I met this lady here and decided to help her first."

Uncle Gideon came out of the back storage closet. When he turned to look at her, the woman lifted her hand.

"Hi."

"Hiya." His uncle was frowning when he turned back to August. "I could've helped her."

"I know, but I've got it."

Gideon took another long look at the woman before grumbling to himself and walking back to the storage room. August knew his uncle was feeling miffed because he worried August didn't need him around anymore. He made a mental note to smooth things over with him later.

"I don't think he likes me," she whispered.

"Don't mind him," August said. "He's irritated with me, not you."

"Hmm."

She didn't look convinced, but who could blame her? Feeling like he needed to save the situation before she walked out the door and never came back, August chuckled. "Now that we, ah, have all that settled, want to tell me who you are and what you need?"

"I'll be h-happy to. My name is Betsy. I'm here visiting for a month and I'd like to take golf lessons."

"*You* want to take lessons?"

"Jah." She narrowed her eyes. "Y-you

don't have a problem with women taking lessons, do you?"

"Nee. I mean, of course not." It was just that her words made him think of a whole list of questions, starting with why she was coming by herself and why she wanted to play when it was obvious that she didn't know the difference between a fairway and a putting green. Finally, he wondered how come she'd picked one of the hottest, most humid, buggiest months of the year to come to Sarasota. Most tourists tried to stay away from the Florida heat.

A line formed in between her perfectly arched dark brown eyebrows. "You don't sound like you mean it."

"I'm just surprised, that's all."

"Why?"

"Well, um, we don't get a lot of women in here wanting to learn to play. Especially not Amish women."

"I guess I . . . I'm the exception to the rule."

He smiled at her. "I'd say so." She was easily five foot seven and slim. She had dark hair, dark eyes, a perfect face. She was beautiful. If she were wearing a pair of shorts and a T-shirt instead of a kapp and dress, some might think she was a model.

"Is there someone who works here who

could teach me? Or, if you don't know of anyone here, do you know where I could take lessons?"

The truth was that they were a public golf course and that was it. The majority of August's days were spent on landscaping, inventory, groundskeeping, and booking tee times. "Well, we don't have a golf pro here."

"What's that?"

"A person who teaches."

Betsy shrugged like that was a minor technicality. "I don't need a pro. I just need someone who doesn't mind teaching an Amish woman the basics of golf."

Gideon popped his head out. "August, could you come help me for a moment?"

There was something in his uncle's voice that he wasn't about to ignore. "Ah, sure. Excuse me, Betsy."

"Of course."

Walking to his uncle, August was sure that he had another reason besides inventory to call him over. He just hoped it wasn't anything too embarrassing. "Yes, Uncle?"

"I think you should teach the girl."

Though August had been thinking the same thing, he was also honest enough to wonder if he was only wanting to teach her so he could be around her longer. "I've never taught anyone to play before."

"That's true. But you're a fine player and a patient one too. You'll do a good job."

"I don't even know what we should charge to teach a beginner."

Uncle Gideon rubbed his beard. "Probably not too much." Looking him over, he added, "I mean, it ain't like you've got much experience with such things."

Hadn't they already just gone over that? "I need to get back to her." Before she decided that he'd left her alone too long and left.

A knowing look entered his uncle's eyes. "Jah, I'd say you do at that, boy."

Flushing, August turned away. Of course his uncle was already seeing hearts and flowers between him and Betsy. Uncle Gideon believed in all those things, thanks to a thirty-year marriage with Diane. It was the opposite of his parents, who had chided him whenever he had thought about anything but duty when he was growing up under their thumbs.

"Sorry about that," he said as he hurried back into the shop. "The course is owned by my aunt and uncle. That's my uncle Gideon. I'm afraid we sometimes let our personal lives get a little too intertwined with our jobs."

"I don't mind. I was looking at all these

accessories. I suppose I'm going to need some of these things?"

He looked around. "A couple. Mainly just a glove."

She smiled in obvious relief. "Oh, gut. I was starting to think that I probably should have taken other things into account besides lesson fees when I decided to take lessons. I-I have a lot of things I need to do this month, you see."

"That sounds intriguing." He paused, hoping she'd take the hint and tell him what in the world she was talking about.

"It's not that interesting, not really." She stood up a little straighter. "So, do you?"

"Do I . . ."

"Know someone who could teach me to play golf?"

He made the decision right then and there. If someone was going to teach Betsy how to swing a golf club, it was going to be him. "Yes. Me."

"You? Don't you have a woman teacher?"

"As I said, we don't have a teacher. We're a small business. And by that, I mean we're real small. Though we have some part-time help, it's mainly just my aunt, my uncle, and me."

"What about your aunt? Maybe she could help me?"

"Sorry, but Aunt Diane doesn't really like to play golf."

"Oh." Betsy continued to look him over like she found him lacking. "Are you sure you don't know of anyone else for me to ask?"

"I could give you the names of some of the other courses around town, but they aren't Amish owned. And they're going to charge you a lot more than I would."

"How do you know?"

"Because I'm going to give you lessons for free."

Betsy looked excited before she seemed to take in the consequences. "Why?"

"Because I think it would be fun to learn how to teach someone, so you can give me that experience. After we're done, I'll be able to tell the next person who comes along that I've taught lessons before."

"Your plan might backfire. I might not be any good at golf."

"Betsy, no one starts out being good at golf. Not even Tiger Woods."

"Who is that?"

"He's a famous golfer." He reached over the counter and picked up the calendar. "When would you like to get started?"

"Tomorrow?"

Scanning the course's bookings, he saw

the usual lull around lunchtime. "Can you take your lesson at noon? I should warn you, though, it's going to be hot."

"I can handle heat. I really do want to learn to play golf." She pursed her lips. "Listen, you're being serious, right? You're not telling me a story about the lessons being free?"

"I'm serious. All you're going to have to do is rent a set of ladies' golf clubs for the month."

"I can't just rent them every time I come in for a lesson?"

"You don't want to do that, girl. That will get expensive," Gideon said as he walked over to join them. "Plus, if you want to learn to play well, you need to get comfortable with one particular set of clubs."

"That makes sense. How much is the rental fee?"

August looked at his uncle. "What do you think?"

"I think we're in the off season and we don't have a lot of female golfers. How does fifty dollars for one month sound, missy?" Gideon asked.

Betsy beamed. "I think it sounds gut. Danke."

"I'll get everything ready for you."

"Should I get one of these gloves too?"

"Jah. Are you right- or left-handed?"

"Right."

"Here's a left glove for you, then. It's ten dollars."

Betsy gave him a ten-dollar bill and put the glove in her purse. "Is that everything?"

"I believe so. I'll be seeing you tomorrow, Betsy."

"Yes. I'll be here at noon." She smiled again.

"I have no doubt that you will."

When she walked out the door, Gideon looked out the window and whistled under his breath. "That woman is a looker, ain't so?"

"She is."

"She's as bright as a new penny too. Sweet but with a touch of vinegar."

August chuckled. "That's a good way to describe her."

Still gazing out the window, Gideon murmured, "So, why does she want to play? Is she aimin' to play with her man or something?"

"I'm not sure. I didn't think to ask." That notion didn't sit real well with him, though. He made a mental note to add it to his list of things to ask her.

He couldn't wait to hear what she had to say.

3

Two hours after Betsy left, Gideon walked up to the counter. "I'll handle things here. You'd best Skype with your mamm and daed. They'll be waiting, you know."

His uncle didn't lie. No doubt his parents were already looking at the clock and wondering how much longer they'd have to wait for him to show up for their scheduled visit. "Danke."

Mentally preparing himself for the upcoming conversation, August walked to the back room that served as both the course's storage area and the employee dining room. In the corner of that space was an ancient computer that Gideon and Diane had reluctantly put in about five years ago after learning that most of their vendors liked to do business on the internet.

To his aunt and uncle's surprise, the appearance of Wi-Fi in the pro shop had brought in an additional number of customers. Now quite a few Englischer golfers came to Snow Bird Golf Course, saying they liked not only the quaint atmosphere and course's design but also being able to use their phones and such when they were checking in or buying things at the pro shop.

Another bonus of the computer and internet connection was the ability for August to Skype with his parents once a month. They didn't have a standing date — his parents' lives as missionaries were too chaotic for that. But usually about three weeks after a Skype session, his mother would email him two choices of days for the following week.

If they were traveling, he'd have to get out the world map to figure out the time zone differences. Eventually, they would agree on a time that wouldn't be in the middle of the night for either of them.

Because they were currently serving in Belize, everything was much easier than it had been when they were in Africa. They were practically in the same time zone. His mother had even commented that they could Skype more often if they weren't so busy.

Ironically, being able to communicate with his parents more frequently wasn't exactly a blessing for August. His parents did not like him working for his aunt and uncle, and they saw no value in taking care of a golf course when he could be doing far loftier work.

He'd long ago given up trying to explain his point of view. Now it was simply easier for him to pretend to be interested in their work while neatly sidestepping questions about his life.

After fortifying himself with an Arnold Palmer — his favorite drink consisting of half iced tea and half lemonade — August sat down, logged into Skype, and waited for the connection to click on.

After two tries, their faces came on the screen. His mother, with her simple wire-rimmed glasses and prematurely gray hair, was wearing a faint smile. Sitting close to her side was his father. His long gray beard, scruffy hair, tan face, and expression of disapproval looked the same as it always did.

August inwardly sighed. Why did his father have to start every conversation with a look of criticism? "Hello, Mamm and Daed."

"Hello to you, August," Mamm said. "You're looking well."

"Danke. You both do too. I hope you are doing fine?"

"I am, but your father has been feeling under the weather of late. Right, David?"

30

His father shrugged. "It's nothing too serious. I must have eaten something that didn't agree with me."

"I'm sorry to hear that."

His father shrugged again. "It's a minor inconvenience, nothing more. It doesn't interfere with our mission to make a difference in people's lives here."

Here we go, August thought. It wasn't that he didn't love the Lord or believe in his parents' good deeds — or even the people they served. It was the way his parents made sure that everyone knew what they were doing. It came off as sanctimonious and — August had come to believe — rather self-serving. His parents had a way of comparing their good deeds to everyone else's — which meant, of course, that they always came off looking the best.

"I hope you'll feel better soon."

"Danke, but my health is hardly worth mentioning. We have much bigger things to worry about than that."

"Oh?"

Daed swallowed, looking like he had just ingested a particularly bitter pill. "Charity, would you like to do the honors or shall I?"

His mother sat up straighter. "I'd be delighted." Looking as excited as a puppy in a roomful of children, she said, "August, we've just heard that we're getting reassigned!"

"Already? You've only been in Belize for seven months. What happened?" Most of their assignments were for two years.

"This is special. The mission in Namibia asked for us specifically."

"The Lord wants us to do our good works there," Daed added.

It took a second for him to place the name with its location. "You're going back to Africa?"

"We are." Mamm gazed at his father with an expression of pure happiness. "We're leaving in three days."

If it were anyone else, August would pepper them with questions.

With his parents, however, almost anything he said would be the wrong thing.

"What will you be doing at the mission?" he felt obliged to ask after an awkward silence.

"Working with some villagers near the coast," his daed answered. "They've recently come into some money from the cruise ships. They've given the organization money to help some of the neediest residents start a clinic and a school."

"We're also going to help women sell their handicrafts to the cruise ship tourists," his mother added. "You know, set up a basic accounting system and make sure that no one is taking advantage of them."

The work would be both interesting and fulfilling. Both of his parents were beaming, probably because of the opportunities and no doubt by the invitation they'd received to be a part of it. "That's amazing. Congratulations."

Right away some of the pleasure in his father's eyes faded. "August, there is nothing to be congratulated about. I am grateful to the Lord for providing so many blessings to these people in Namibia."

Why hadn't he kept his mouth shut? "Of course you are."

"The glory always goes to God, August," Mamm chided. "You mustn't ever forget that."

He gritted his teeth but nodded. "I won't, Mamm."

Narrowing her eyes, she somehow managed to look down on him even through a screen half a world away. "It's no wonder that you often forget His good works, living the way you do in Florida."

Let it go, a small voice whispered to him.

Usually he heeded that voice. Today, August didn't feel like it. "What's that supposed to mean?"

His mother's eyes widened. His father, on the other hand, scowled. "Don't play games, son. We both know that your life on the golf course is nothing less than shameful."

And there it was. More condemnation and disparagement, all wrapped up in a tidy sentence. He was tired of getting put down for not following in their footsteps. "It's always been amazing to me that you both can be completely accepting of everyone who you work with, no matter their pasts. Yet here I am, working five and six days a week at a perfectly respectable job with Daed's sister and her husband and yet you act as if I've sinned terribly."

"Don't make light of such things, August," Daed said.

"I'm not. I just think you need to learn to accept my life too." And that was the key word — accept. Not proud or even happy for him. Was he really asking for so much?

Tears formed in his mother's eyes. "August, we are only able to converse with you once every few weeks. I'm disappointed that you had to ruin it. On a day when we had such wonderful news to share too."

"So this is all my fault?"

His father's glare looked as cold as it used to when August was twelve and thirteen. "I think it's time we got off Skype," he said. "I suggest you pray about your treatment of your mother."

What had he done to his mamm? "What are you talking about? How did I treat Mamm badly?"

"I'm not going to justify your rudeness with a reply."

"But Daed —"

"We are disappointed in you. Next month, when we're in our new home, I hope you will be more respectful."

August felt some of the last vestiges of hope in his heart fade. Though he hadn't thought things between him and his parents would ever change, conversations like they'd just exchanged illustrated how much they weren't going to. "I wish you safe travels," he said in a soft voice. "May God be with you."

"Danke, August," his mother said softly.

Then they disconnected.

Staring at the blank screen, he felt tears prick his eyes. They'd ended the conversation without saying that they loved him. That was a long-standing manipulation of theirs — and it was one of the first lessons he'd learned from them when he was small. If he didn't behave, they wouldn't tell him that they loved him at night. When he was a little boy, he used to live in fear of dying in

35

his sleep without his parents' love.

He still resented the game they'd played with his heart.

Though August respected his parents' mission work and loved them, he didn't like them all that much.

He didn't like the way he became whenever he was around his parents either: hard and bitter, like all his edges became jagged and torn.

It wasn't the way he wanted to be. He wanted to be a man he could be proud of. A man the woman in his life would be proud to call hers.

The type of man to never hold his love apart for the mere reason that he wanted to be right.

Those were things to aspire to, he thought.

He just needed to make sure he remembered that when sleep evaded him in the middle of the night.

4

Feeling confused and not ready to tell Mary about her trip to the golf course, Betsy got on the SCAT and rode to Siesta Key. The half-hour ride to the small island just off the shore gave her plenty of time to think about her upcoming lessons, and August Troyer, and how goofy she'd acted from the moment she'd walked through the golf course's front entrance.

It just went to show that *imagining* things and *experiencing* the reality could be far different. Almost getting hit by that golf ball had been exactly what she needed to wake up and realize that she not only needed to be brave to work on this life list of hers, but she needed to be smart about it too. Otherwise, she was going to get hurt and likely be covered with bruises.

Thinking about the narrow miss and August's almost-rescue, she had to smile. *Thank you, God,* she prayed silently. *Not only did You keep me from harm, but You also did it with enough* umph *to catch my attention.*

The Lord was probably shaking His head at her too. Time and again Betsy had been told that she had such tunnel vision that she forgot to look around her to see what else was going on.

"You must be thinking of a good memory," the woman across the aisle from her said with a wry smile.

Betsy hadn't even realized the English woman was there. Turning to get a better look at her, she first noticed a pair of tan legs in crisp white shorts, a black tank top, and black leather sandals. She also had short, curly brown hair, matching brown eyes, and a kind smile. Everything about her seemed nice and friendly.

"I-I was," she answered at last. "Well, it was a good memory and also something of a much-needed jolt, I suppose."

"A jolt?"

"Jah. You see . . . I almost got hit by a golf ball this morning."

The woman's brown eyes widened before she chuckled. "Out of all the things I could have imagined you saying, that wasn't one of them."

"Since I never thought I would be standing in the way of a bunch of golfers, I'd say you and I are on the same page."

"Where are you off to now?"

"The beach." Seeing that the driver had already crossed the narrow stretch of waterway, she added, "The first stop is soon."

Humor lit the woman's eyes. "I guess that was a silly question. This is the Siesta Key shuttle."

"It's not silly. Learning which SCAT bus goes where takes some time." Betsy smiled at her again. "I just arrived here two days ago. Are you a visitor too?"

"Yes. I came to Florida with my sister."

"That's nice."

Something in the woman's eyes faded. "Yes, it is."

Betsy wondered why the woman didn't seem too happy but then reflected that it was likely none of her business. Instead, she spent the rest of the time looking out the window and people watching.

"First Siesta Key stop!" the driver called out.

Over half the occupants in the bus stood up and filed out. The woman she was talking to as well. "My name is Annie," she said as she waited for the line to move. "It feels funny not to give you my name after you've been so nice to chat with."

"I'm Betsy."

"It's good to meet you. Will you be here for a while?"

"A whole month."

Annie's smile widened. "Me too. Maybe we'll see each other again, then."

"Yes. I hope so."

"Well, I better get on my way." She joined the line of people, most of whom were holding foam noodles, towels, and beach bags, and eventually got off.

From her seat, Betsy watched Annie pause on the sidewalk to get her bearings before following the rest of the group through the parking lot to the beach.

Ten minutes later, she was doing the same thing, only in a far less crowded spot. Jayson had once told her, Mary, and Lilly about the "other" beach to visit. They'd all been so happy to learn about where the locals went.

Thinking of the way he'd obviously been attracted to Mary from the start, Betsy wondered if Mary had felt the same way.

Was that what love was? A chance meeting, followed by an instant connection? Or had that just been happenstance for Mary and Jayson? Betsy supposed it didn't matter. He and Mary had fallen in love after a bit of a rocky start and now were starting their own family.

40

For an instant, Betsy thought about August again — before firmly pushing away the fanciful thought. He was not her future — he was just a man who was patient and kind.

That was it.

Taking a deep breath and deciding that her lungs were doing just fine, she let her mind drift toward other things.

Such as the fact that it was time for her to think about the rest of her list and to make some more plans. She walked to the little hut that sold snacks and drinks, bought a soft serve ice cream cone, and then sat down on one of the folding chairs. She would've preferred to sit on the sand, but she hadn't brought a towel. Yet again, she was unprepared.

Annie Jackson was a lot of things. She was a pretty good singer, decent at organizing things, and exceptional at stretching a dollar. She also enjoyed learning about history and, consequently, was awfully good at trivia games. What she was not, unfortunately, was a very good companion to her older sister, Danielle.

In a burst of weakness and sympathy, Annie had agreed to join Danielle on a month's vacation on Longboat Key, just north of

Sarasota. With anyone else, the chance to escape her cramped condo in Cincinnati for a month of lounging by the pool, eating out, and exploring the area would sound like the vacation of a lifetime.

With Danielle, the experience was anything but that. Her sister's divorce had just been finalized and she was still extremely bitter about it. She had two grown children who didn't speak to her and an ex-husband who seemed to be perpetually celebrating that she was out of his life.

It wasn't very kind to say, but sometimes Annie could understand where Peter was coming from. Simply put, Danielle wasn't easy. She never had been, either. Her recent divorce had increased her poor attitude.

Her older sister also had a lot of money — thanks to the fact that she'd invested a good chunk of the money she made as a real estate agent in the nineties.

Now Danielle didn't do much of anything. She didn't work — not at a job and not at home. Instead, her sister employed a variety of people to do things for her. Instead of doing them herself or helping, she monitored their efforts.

Annie imagined that just about everyone Danielle employed quickly learned that working for her was a thankless job. She

found fault with pretty much everything —
which meant she was either hiring, training,
criticizing, or firing everyone in her life.

Except for Annie.

In most ways, she and Annie were exact
opposites. First off, Annie had never married. Oh, she'd been in love. She'd fallen in
love during college, but Clay had ultimately
decided that he'd rather join the army than
meld his life with hers. She'd been heartbroken at the loss. Five years later, she'd been
heartbroken again when she'd learned that
he'd died on a mission overseas.

Secondly, although Annie had worked
hard too, she'd never made tons of money
to invest in the stock market. Annie had
taught high school history for about a
decade, then worked as a secretary in a law
firm. Now, she had a blog about ways to
make a dollar go further. That had been
something of a surprise — especially since
her money-saving tips were actually making
her more money than teaching or secretarial
work ever had.

Now, at forty-five years of age, she figured
she was living a pretty good life. She did
her blog and YouTube videos, ran a couple
of times a week, read books, and simply
enjoyed being in charge of her own schedule.

She must have been experiencing a moment of weakness when Danielle had called and asked if she would join her on vacation.

For a brief moment it had sounded so fun and exciting.

Annie had started regretting the decision from the moment Danielle cried when their plane was delayed, cried when one of her four suitcases hadn't made the connection, and cried when they got to the villa and discovered that the house next door was under construction.

There were only so many tears Annie could take.

So she'd begun to spend a lot more of her days by herself. Which was why she was currently sitting on a towel on the beach in Siesta Key and not next to her sister on a lounge chair next to the pool.

When her cell phone rang, she reluctantly glanced at the screen then answered when she saw it was her niece Phil. Phil was short for Ophelia — which Phil had decided was too fancy of a name back when she was about eight years old.

"Hi, Phil."

"Hey, Aunt Annie. What's going on?" She lowered her voice. "You're not with Mom right now, are you?"

She couldn't help but smile. Phil sounded

as wary as if she were asking if there were a tribe of zombies wandering nearby. "I am not. I'm actually sitting on a beach towel on Siesta Key."

"Is that near the house?"

"Kind of. It's just a short shuttle ride from there. You'd love this beach. The sand is pure white and feels like sugar."

"It sounds great. So . . . where is Mom?"

"Still at the house. Well, she was last time I checked."

"Okay, good."

"Uh, why?" She knew Danielle wasn't easy, but she hadn't imagined that Phil would sound so worried about being overheard.

"I wanted to talk to you."

Which told her nothing. "Why? Honey, is everything okay?"

"Yeah. I was just worried about you." She paused. "Are you miserable?"

"I'm fine."

"Travis and I were talking, and we decided that you're probably not. Mom can get pretty mean when she isn't getting enough attention. And no offense, Annie, but you're never going to be able to give her enough attention."

"Oh, Phil. I'm sorry." Though Annie knew her sister could be a handful, it made her so sad that her sweet daughter rarely saw the other, warmer side of her mother.

"Nothing for you to be sorry about. I just wanted to make sure that you weren't thinking that you had to stay with her for a whole month if she was making you sad. You don't have to, you know," she added quickly. "Mom is far more capable than she lets on. The moment you leave, she'll be on the phone inviting someone else to join her."

Though Annie figured Phil's words were true, the sentiment behind them was certainly painful to hear. "Honey, I can take care of myself. I promise. You don't need to worry about me. Now, why don't you tell me what brought this on?"

"Travis and I had lunch with Dad yesterday, and he got a mean text from Mom."

"Peter did?"

"Oh yeah. The text was so long and it was all about how she was lonely, you weren't all that helpful, and that nothing in her house was very nice."

Annie rolled her eyes. "I had no idea that she still texted Peter."

"Dad gets texts from her all the time. He says he can't block her in case something happens with Travis or me." Phil paused, then added, "Travis is worried that she has you carrying all her bags and stuff. You

46

know, like one of those paid companions in a Jane Austen movie."

The idea of her nephew even knowing about such things made her giggle. "My arms aren't sore yet, Phil."

"See, Aunt Annie, the three of us started talking and we all really feel like you need a support group this month."

"A support group?"

"You know, like you could call a friend if Mom makes you so mad you feel like throwing something at her."

Annie couldn't help it, she laughed. "I haven't felt like launching anything at your mother yet, but if I feel the urge, I'll call you. I promise."

"Call any of us. Dad, Travis, or even Jeff."

"Thank you. I hope I won't have to call your husband, though. Feel free to pass the word that I'm fine. Danielle hasn't driven me batty yet."

"Okay. But look out for when she goes on a rant."

"I promise, I've known Danielle a lot longer than you have. I'm used to her silliness."

"Just know that we love you."

"Are you sure you don't want to give her a call and tell her the same thing? Your mom would probably love to hear that."

"Annie, last time I called Mom, all she did was talk bad about Jeff and how I've gained weight since I got married."

"I'm sorry."

"Me too. I know everyone says I should give her a break because she's going through a hard time, but I don't know why I have to put up with her putting me down."

"I don't think you have to put up with her snipes at all. And don't worry about me."

"Let me know when you're home and I'll come see you."

"Okay, sweetheart."

After they hung up, she sighed. Annie wasn't sure what had happened to her sister to make her so unpleasant, but she supposed she should stop trying to figure it out. Danielle hadn't been all that nice when they were in school and now was pretty much a spoiled brat.

Stuffing her phone in her bag, Annie decided to put her sister out of her mind for the next five hours. It was why she'd come to the beach after all. She needed a break.

She contemplated getting out her book but that meant switching to reading glasses. Instead, she stretched out her legs, scanned the area, and then finally settled in to watch the big family to her right.

Like her, they weren't Amish, but they did seem to have a close bond. They had a big setup too. Beach cabana, coolers, beach chairs, toys for the kids. Lots of kids and at least two couples, along with a few extra guys who seemed to be there to tease the kids and buy them treats.

One man in particular had caught her eye. He was around her age, was wearing a pair of board shorts and sunglasses. He was also — she couldn't help but notice — in really good shape. All the kids circled around him, smiling up at him like he was the star attraction at the beach.

When a pair of kids pretended to sneak up on him, he turned and grabbed their ankles instead. The children squealed. He laughed.

And in spite of her attempt to watch him in an un-creepy way, Annie laughed too.

That's when he turned to look at her.

She'd been caught staring.

Deciding that she might as well own up to it, Annie smiled. "Sorry, it was just so fun to see you be as sneaky as the kids."

"I've got to be on my A game or I won't stand a chance," he joked. "Hey, I hope our crew isn't bothering you. We took over this space when you were already set up."

She gestured to her printed beach bag and

towel. "Obviously, it didn't take me too long to get set up. If I wanted to move, I would."

"Okay. Well, I would say that we'll probably get quieter as the day goes on, but that's doubtful. The bunch of us tend to get loud when we're around each other."

She liked that he seemed to be completely at ease with his family. It was such a nice contrast from hers. "That's how it should be, right?"

"Yeah." He smiled at her.

When he didn't look in any hurry to turn away, Annie decided to ask another question. "Are you all here on vacation?"

"We are. I live in Toledo."

"I'm from Cincinnati."

"You down here with family too?"

"My sister. She rented a villa over on Longboat Key and asked me to join her."

He whistled low. "That's a really beautiful area. I bet it's awesome."

"It is. Everything on Longboat is pretty."

"Well, we're all staying at the Sandy Shores Motel." He grinned. "It's kind of the opposite of a Longboat Key villa."

"Is that nearby?"

"Yeah. Picture a Pepto-pink 1970s-style motel. Now picture the fact that it's clean but most of the furnishings are from that era too."

She playfully winced. "Oh. I hope you have a decent mattress at least."

"Not really, but it's just for a week. My sister found the place and the price was right for all of us to take it over."

"That sounds fun."

"You know what? It has been."

"Jack?" One of the women was calling out to him.

"I'm coming, Cara." Looking sheepish, he stood up. "I've been summoned to help with bathroom shuttling. It was nice to meet you . . ."

"Annie."

His smile widened. "Annie. I'm Jack. Maybe I'll see you around."

"Maybe." She watched him grab two little boys' hands and walk them down to the bathrooms. One of the little boys had to skip to keep up with Jack's long legs.

As they faded from sight, Annie bit back a feeling of disappointment. She wished she could've found a guy like that. Someone who was friendly and easygoing. Good with kids and large families. Who didn't need everything to be top of the line with a prestigious name.

She would've liked that. No, she would've liked that a lot.

Frustrated with herself, she flipped over

on her stomach and tried to concentrate on her tan.

"You need to count your blessings too," she muttered to herself. Sitting around wishing for things to be different wasn't any way to live.

She'd learned that a long time ago.

5

Betsy had risen just as the sun rose on the horizon. After reading her daily devotional, she'd taken a shower and put on one of her coolest dresses. She'd hummed to herself while she made her bed and smiled at her reflection in the bathroom mirror while she pulled up her hair and pinned on a kapp. By the time she walked down the hall to the kitchen, she practically felt like singing. At last, she was going to do something on her life list. She felt optimistic and happy and proud of herself.

Until Mary had greeted her, handed her a cup of coffee, and started asking questions.

"Are you sure you want to play golf today?" she asked. "It's awfully warm."

"Of course I'm sure. I have a lesson scheduled. Besides, it's not that warm."

"The temperature is going to get a lot hotter by the time you get over to the golf course."

"I'm sure it will be warmer, but it's just a golf lesson, ain't so? I'll likely be spending most of my time listening to August show me how to swing a golf club."

"It's still exercise."

"I'll be fine," Betsy said. "Lots of people play golf when it's hot out, Mary."

"I know that, but usually it's men in slacks or shorts and a golf shirt and women in shorts or golf dresses."

"Golf dresses?"

Mary waved a hand like Betsy was getting stuck on a technicality. "You know what I mean. The women wear short dresses out of a cool, knit material. You're in a long dress."

"I am, but it's a cool, loose-fitting one."

"Still . . ."

Betsy felt like rolling her eyes. "I'm still Amish, you know. These dresses pretty much come with the territory."

"All I'm saying is that dress might make it hard to swing a golf club."

Though Mary likely had a point, Betsy was going to do the best she could. "I'm pretty certain it's going to be hard for me to swing a golf club no matter what I'm wearing," she joked. "I don't think wearing a pair of shorts will improve my swing." She poured herself another cup of coffee and eyed the two pieces of bread she'd just placed in the toaster.

Mary took butter and jam out of the refrigerator, along with a bowl of fresh fruit. "You didn't sign up for a bunch of lessons, did you? Because —"

"Mary, what has gotten into you? Ever since I arrived and told you about my list, you've come up with all kinds of concerns and warnings." When her girlfriend looked guilty, Betsy became even more confused. "What happened to the girl I knew last year who was up for anything? Back when we were stuck in a motel room in the middle of Georgia, you never acted like everything had to be perfect."

Her girlfriend bit her lip. "Oh my word, I've been doing that, haven't I? I'm so sorry." Looking even more frazzled, she said, "Your toast is done. You should put butter on it before it cools."

Betsy did as she suggested and added a generous amount of locally made orange marmalade. "I don't want an apology. Instead, I'd rather you tell me what you're so worried about."

"I'm not supposed to say."

Betsy groaned. "Did you hear from my mother again?"

Looking even guiltier, Mary nodded. "Jah."

"Did she call or write?"

"She called."

She took her toast and a small bowl of fruit to the table and sat down. "When did my mother call?"

Like a suspect getting interrogated, her friend cracked under the pressure. "This morning." She sat down at the table next to her. "I'm so sorry, Betsy. I can't not answer when your mother calls."

"I know."

"Plus, I don't know how to not listen when your mother starts telling me about everything Jayson and I need to worry about."

Taking a bite of toast, Betsy stewed. She hadn't come to Mary and Jayson's in order to be watched over. Even thinking about Mary getting a list of concerns from her mother was horrifying. "I can't believe my mamm called and she didn't want to talk to me."

"Well . . . I'm pretty sure that she doesn't think you'll listen to her." Mary sipped her water.

So her mother decided to pester Mary instead. Her parents' interference was getting ridiculous. "That's it. I'm going to call her right now."

Mary's eyes widened. "Oh, I really wish

you wouldn't. She's going to be upset that I told you."

All that meant to her was that her mother was determined to continue to be sneaky. "Hearing that she never intended for me to find out what she was doing makes everything even worse. This isn't okay, Mary. Not for me or for you."

"Well, um, okay."

Betsy wasn't positive but she was pretty sure she detected a hint of relief in her eyes. "You don't mind if I use your kitchen phone, do you?" Since they were New Order Amish, Mary and Jayson had a phone, but it was a landline in the kitchen.

"Of course I don't mind. But, ah, try not to get too irate, okay? I really think your mother's actions came from her heart."

Betsy smiled at her. "I won't."

As she walked out of the room, Mary called out, "You won't get too irate or you won't try not to get that way?"

"Both!" Glad that she'd found the source of the tension between them, Betsy finished her toast and fruit, rinsed off her dishes, then at last picked up the phone. She would call her mother, tell her to stop nagging Mary, then start on her way to the golf course.

Five minutes later, it was obvious to Betsy

that the conversation wasn't going to be nearly as easy as she'd hoped.

Actually, she was gritting her teeth while her mother pretended that she hadn't been asking Mary for Betsy's health reports on the sly.

"You need to tell me the truth, Mamm. Not another fib."

After her mother seemed to get over her shock, she shared a long, convoluted story about a mud sale she was organizing. "So that's what I've been doing," she finished with a fake laugh. "Now, why don't you fill me in about your vacation, Elizabeth? You know, we've hardly talked."

"Mamm, there's no need to tell you much since you've been sneaking around behind my back and calling Mary."

"I haven't been sneaking." Her voice was a good two octaves too high.

"You've been corresponding with Mary without my knowledge. You've been asking her for reports about me. If that isn't sneaking, I don't know what is."

"It's not sneaking."

"Fine. How would you describe your behavior? Simple lying?"

"Don't raise your voice at me."

"Well, don't you ask Mary questions about my personal life. It's very rude."

"Betsy —"

She cut her off. "Mamm, besides the fact that what you were doing was wrong, you've put Mary in a really tough position. She isn't comfortable lying to me and she also isn't happy about having to tattle on me."

"I've been reduced to doing these things because you haven't been calling me."

"Mamm. What is it going to take to get you to understand that you aren't making things easier? Instead of helping me, you're making things harder. You aren't listening and you're being sneaky. All I want to do is stay away for as long as possible — and ignore your phone calls."

"You better not do that."

"I will if you don't settle down."

"If you were in my position, you'd understand why I'm doing the things I'm doing, daughter." Hurt laced every word.

Betsy covered her face with her hand as she tried to remain calm. "I feel the same way. If you saw your actions from my point of view, you would feel stifled." She exhaled. "Mamm, I'm serious. You've got to give me some space. If you can't do that, then I'm afraid our relationship is going to suffer."

"It sounds like you're giving me an ultimatum."

"All I'm doing is standing up for myself.

There's a difference."

"Fine." Her mother didn't sound convinced.

"I mean it. I'm a grown woman and I'm used to dealing with my lungs a whole lot more than you are. I know when they get tight, and I take medicine. I also know when I need to take a break. I don't want to get sick any more than you do."

"I understand."

"Does that mean you'll stop calling Mary and asking for reports?"

"It means I will try."

Well, at least she was telling her the truth. "That's not good enough. I want you to promise me that you'll stop interfering so much."

"Elizabeth, you're making quite a fuss. Where did you get this stubbornness from? I must say that I'm rather taken aback."

Betsy giggled. "Oh, Mamm. I think we both know where I got my stubbornness. It sure didn't come from Daed."

"I suppose that is true." Humor laced her tone as well. "So, you're off to your golf lesson this morning?"

"I am." Glancing at the clock, she winced. "I've got to go or I'll be late."

"All right. Well, um, have a good time."

"Danke, Mamm. I love you."

"I love you too, dear."

After she hung up and reassured Mary that she hadn't lost her cool, Betsy picked up her tote bag, double-checked that her refillable water bottle, sunscreen, and new golf glove were inside, and hurried over to Snow Bird Golf Course. It took her fifteen minutes. She was on time, but just barely.

When she entered the pro shop, August was behind the counter checking in a pair of Amish men in their forties. He glanced her way and smiled before giving them their change.

"Hiya, Betsy. You ready to play some golf?"

The golfers stared at her in surprise.

"Are ya golfing today?" one asked.

"Nee. I'm just taking some lessons."

They stared at her in confusion, then one of them smiled. "You'd best start giving us a warning if young women are going to be let loose on the course, August."

"I'd give you a warning, but I'm sure she's going to be doing so well that you two will be asking her to join ya for a round before too long."

The other golfer tipped his hat at her. "I hope this young man is right, missy. You'll brighten up the greenery just fine."

She giggled at their audaciousness.

After they left, August came around the

61

counter. "Ready to give golf a try?"

"I am. I'm excited. And a little nervous. I have a feeling I'm going to make a fool of myself."

"Don't worry about that. You won't make a fool of yourself, and besides, everyone has been where you are. No one is born knowing how to swing a golf club."

She smiled at him, liking the way he was being encouraging but not making any false promises.

"Okay, here's what I did." He pulled out a blue folder and then, to her surprise, pulled out a golf bag too. "I printed out some basic information about golf, got you a folder so you can write down notes, and outfitted a bag for you too."

"Thank you."

"Of course. Now, let's head to the driving range."

When he made a move to pick up her bag, she held him off. "No you don't. I'm the golfer. I can carry my own clubs just like everyone else."

He looked doubtful but shrugged. "All right. Let's go."

Lifting up the bag on one shoulder, she paused as her body adjusted to the weight.

August raised his eyebrows. "Are you okay? Would you like a push cart?"

Maybe she should be accepting that offer, but she was still stinging from the conversation with her mother. Looking out at the golfers congregating near the carts, she noticed that about half of the men were carrying their clubs. Only the older men were either using the golf carts or pushing their golf bags.

"I'm fine," she said with a tight smile as she followed him out of the pro shop.

Of course, ten steps in, as she walked with August to the driving range in the hot Floridian sun, Betsy began to wonder if she was in over her head.

And that maybe — just maybe — both Mary and her mother had been right to be a little worried about her.

The clubs were heavy and clanked against her side. Carrying them with any sort of grace was harder than it looked.

It was also very warm, she was sweating, and she would've paid money to be wearing a much shorter dress that didn't keep getting tangled in her legs as they walked.

"You still okay?" August asked.

"Oh jah. I'm fine."

August looked doubtful but didn't say a word.

She hoped he would never realize just how much she was struggling. If he did, he might decide that teaching her to play golf was a little more than he wanted to take on.

She wouldn't blame him one bit, either.

6

August was beginning to realize that teaching Betsy how to play golf wasn't going to be as easy as he thought. Actually, within their first couple of minutes together, he came to the conclusion that it was going to be really hard.

The first problem was that he often became tongue-tied around her. Betsy had a sweet, rather adorable stutter that appeared when she got nervous. It turned his insides to mush. Whenever she fumbled over a word, he wanted to reassure her and make her feel better.

Then, to make matters worse, she stared at him like he could be on the PGA tour. He found himself spouting stupid bits of information just to impress her.

In addition, she was one of the prettiest girls he'd been around. August was used to playing golf with other guys and joking around. Now he found himself staring at her dark hair and comparing its sheen to a raven's wings. He was pretty horrified about that.

However, the biggest problem was that Betsy was the worst golfer he'd ever met.

Actually, it was kind of a surprise just how unathletic she seemed to be. He'd been around inexperienced golfers plenty of times. He'd also been around lots of women possessing various degrees of athletic prowess — or at least some coordination.

That said, most people on a golf course had held a golf club before or swung either a tennis racket or baseball bat in the past. Or they were golf fans.

Betsy was none of those things. She was as comfortable with a 9 iron in her hands as she might have been holding a wasp's nest. She didn't understand any golfing terms and hadn't even been on a course before — not counting the time she had wandered through his.

As pitiful of a golfer as she was, at least her attitude was good. Betsy seemed to be really enjoying herself. She smiled the entire time — kind of the way a puppy looks when it's allowed to roam about on the beach without a leash.

Most people put pressure on themselves to do well. Betsy, on the other hand, acted as if being at the golf course was enough. If she could only make contact with a little white ball more often, they'd be on a roll. Or, um, on the fairway.

After she swung again, making a kind of albatrossy dip and swoop as she followed through, August stepped closer. "Maybe we should revisit the basic golf swing?" he suggested.

"Are you sure?" Betsy started to swing the 9 iron back — and almost hit him in the head.

He darted out of her way just in time. "Watch it, Betsy. You're swinging a potential weapon!"

She pivoted to face him, still with that blasted 9 iron in her grip. "Sorry!"

"It's okay. Just, ah, be careful." He motioned with his hands. "Stand still, I need to come closer."

"Oh, brother."

She did turn as still as a statue, though, for which he was both relieved and amused. After pulling the club from her hands, he said, "Shake them out." When she shook her hands a bit, he lowered his chin so their eyes could meet. "Now, do you remember your grip and the placement of your thumbs?"

"Jah. I mean, I kind of do."

Carefully, he rearranged her fingers. "There you go. Now, take a moment and look at your grip. Close your eyes and think about how it feels." He moved to the side. "Swing it gently, just back and forth."

Betsy did as he asked. "What am I supposed to be thinking now?"

"That this is the way you should be holding the club. Can you tell that this feels almost familiar? You know, that your hands are gripping the club naturally?"

"Nee. None of this feels familiar or natural, August."

He laughed. "I can see why you might think it, but you're doing better. I promise you that." Okay, that was a lie, but he didn't want to hurt her feelings.

"Now what?"

"Now we're going to continue to work on your swing." As she moved, he put his hands on her hips. "Now shift your weight. Easily."

She practiced with his new directions, finally beaming. "I think I'm better."

"I think you are too," he teased.

Looking up at him, she blushed. "Maybe you don't need to still be holding on to me?"

"Hmm?" Only then did he realize that he'd been standing there with his hands on her hips.

On her hips!

He dropped his hands like they'd been burned — which was a good comparison since his cheeks seemed to be flaming with embarrassment. "I'm so sorry. I don't know what I was thinking." Or, well, maybe he did know what he was thinking . . . but she sure didn't need to know that!

Her pretty brown eyes widened as she stared at him.

That smile she'd been wearing had vanished. August drew in a deep breath, afraid he'd completely offended her. Worse, creeped her out, like he was some kind of man who enjoyed getting cheap thrills at his student's expense. A dozen words of apology came to mind, each one sounding more trite or vaguely condescending than the last.

And then she laughed.

The noise floated down the range, making more than one golfer freeze or lift his head up.

"Sorry," she apologized after a moment. "I have a feeling that laughing so loud is probably another mistake I just made. I'll try to be quieter."

"I've heard all kinds of talk, joking, and laughter around here. Golfing is a sport, but it's a social one. No one expects a player to be completely quiet or a pro. It's a game, jah?"

Betsy nodded. "I-I suppose it is. I never thought about it all that much."

Her comment surprised him, mainly because if she hadn't been thinking about actually going out and playing eighteen holes, then what had she been thinking about?

"We're almost out of time. How about you hit another six balls and then we'll call it a day?"

"All right."

She moved a ball onto the tee, nibbled on her bottom lip as she arranged her hands, then swung.

And then, just as if the Lord had decided to take pity on her — or maybe simply give her the boost she needed — her ball went sailing through the air. Passed a number of markers, and at last landed near the two-hundred-yard marker.

August couldn't help but gape. That shot had been a thing of beauty. The slight *thunk* when her club hit the ball had been perfect. The ball had flown through the air straight and sure.

She turned to face him, looking stunned. "August, did you see that?"

"I did." He glanced out at the driving

range as if he could really see which ball had been hers. "I'm real proud of you. Good job!"

"Danke." Her eyes were wide and bright. And dancing.

He was mesmerized. For a second, he even considered pulling her close. Maybe twirling her around. Neither of which was a good idea.

Like, not at all.

"You know what? I think maybe it would be best if we stopped right now."

She frowned. "You don't want me to hit five more balls?"

"Nee. You might hit all of them that well . . . but you might not. What do you think?"

"I think it's a pretty good possibility that I won't."

"When you leave here, I want you to be feeling pleased with yourself. And, of course, to want to take another lesson."

She chuckled. "Are you sure you want me to come back?"

"Oh yeah." He cleared his throat. "I mean, of course. After all, that's why I'm here, ain't so?"

Betsy nodded, but her expression looked thoughtful. With obvious care, she slipped the 9 iron back in her golf bag, pulled off

71

her glove, and then hoisted the bag onto her shoulder. "I think I'm ready now."

He reached out and took the bag from her shoulder and shrugged it onto his shoulder instead. When she looked to protest, he said, "I don't mind, Betsy. Now, come on. I'll walk you back."

As she fell into step beside him, everything in his life seemed to slide into place. It was silly — he barely knew the girl and it had only been one golf lesson, after all.

But a part of him was certain that the Lord hadn't just been at work making golf balls sail through the air . . . He'd also been working on August's life. Showing him that he hadn't been making mistakes by working for his aunt and uncle. He hadn't been wrong to try to go his own way.

The Lord had a path for every person, no matter how important or forgettable.

Right at this moment, carrying Betsy's clubs, everything felt right in the world.

He hoped that feeling would last a little while longer. It was too beautiful of a feeling not to hold on to as long as he could.

7

Betsy couldn't stop smiling. She'd done it. No matter what else happened during the rest of her vacation, she'd accomplished at least one thing on her life list. She had found a golf course, signed up for lessons, and then taken her first one. She was so proud of herself.

August seemed to be happy with how her first lesson went too. "You did great, Betsy," he said as they walked back to the pro shop. He was graciously carrying her bag, saying that it was the least he could do since she'd done so well.

"Danke, August." She thought he was laying the praise on a bit thick since she had only had a couple of decent shots and only one great one, but she didn't try to take her bag from him. It was hot and some of her muscles were already feeling a bit sore. Swinging golf clubs was more of a workout than she'd imagined.

"Don't forget that you need to practice hitting balls at least one time before your next lesson," he warned.

"I won't forget."

"Good. We'll have you out on the course in no time."

"Do you really think so?"

"I do." Looking as confident as he sounded, August continued. "I think getting to actually play a round is going to help your golf swing. You'll certainly enjoy it more. It's a lot more fun than just hitting balls at the driving range."

She grinned up at him. "Since my goal is to play at least one round of golf, I would like that very much."

"Next time, maybe after you practice on the driving range, I'll take you over to the putting green and you can practice there too."

"I should do much better on the putting green. I've played miniature golf quite a few times." Well, she'd played three times and had come in last place each time, but August didn't need to know that.

"For some reason, that doesn't surprise me."

"Oh?"

"You don't seem like the type of woman who never gets out to do fun things."

Thinking of all the times she had been the observer instead of a participant, she muttered, "If only that were true."

"Wait, that hasn't been the case?" When she shook her head, he gazed at her another long second. "Hmm. It sounds like there's a story there."

"There is a little bit of one." Not that she was going to share it with him, though. They were almost back at the pro shop. And she wasn't exactly anxious to tell August all about her health issues.

Right before they went inside, August paused. "Hey, Betsy, are you in a hurry to go home?"

"Not really. Why?"

"Well, um, would you like to get a sandwich or some lunch?"

"You're asking me out to lunch?"

He set her bag on the ground. "Well, jah." He took off his hat and ran his fingers through his hair. "I mean, I think I just did. What do you think?"

She thought that going out to lunch with him sounded like a whole lot more fun than going back to Mary's house. Mary was either going to want to take a nap or pepper her with questions about how her lungs felt. "I think that sounds like a lot of fun. Danke."

He grinned under his straw hat. "Come on in. I'll get you something to drink while I check in with my aunt and uncle."

Betsy followed him inside and stood off to the side as a woman in a turquoise dress, yellow rubber flip-flops, and a bright smile greeted August.

"How did the lesson go, August? Any problems?"

August shared a smile with Betsy as he handed her a bottle of water. "I don't think so. Betsy is a quick learner."

The woman turned to face her. "I'm sorry. I didn't even see you standing there. I'm Diane."

"I'm Betsy. It's nice to meet you." She unscrewed the cap and took a long sip of ice-cold water. Of course it went straight to her brain, but the cold liquid did taste wonderful after being out so long in the hot sun.

Diane's smile widened. "Same. Do you think you'll come back?"

"I do. I have another lesson in five or six days. Eventually I want to be able to play a whole round of golf."

Diane folded her hands behind her back. "What else are you planning to do on your vacation?" She winked. "It's too hot to play golf every day."

"I'm staying with a girlfriend. I'll spend time with her, but I'm going to do some other things too. I have a list of things I want to accomplish while I'm here."

August walked to her side. "She's going to tell me all about it while we have lunch today."

August's uncle popped his head out of the back room. "You're going to take off for lunch, August?"

"I am. I'll be back in an hour, though, all right?"

"Of course it's all right. You can even stay longer if you want," Diane said. "Enjoy your lunch, kids."

Betsy felt her cheeks heat up again. "Danke."

If August felt uncomfortable about his aunt's comment, he didn't show it. "Would you two like me to bring you anything back from the sub shop?"

"Just yourself," Diane said with a smile.

"Come on, Betsy, let's get out of here." He held open the door for her and followed her out.

As they walked down the cart path toward the entrance, someone called out, "Fore!"

When she stopped to see who was yelling at them, August wrapped an arm around her shoulders as he pulled her behind him.

A golf ball landed with a *thunk* just about five feet away. If August hadn't moved so quickly, she would've gotten hit, for sure and for certain. "That was another close call."

"Jah. Are you all right?" He searched her face.

"Oh jah." She smiled. "I tell you what, August. I had no idea golf was such a dangerous sport."

"I never thought it was either, but now I'm starting to think it can be really dangerous if a person ain't careful."

"I obviously need to be more careful. Thank you for keeping me so safe around here."

"It's nothing."

"It wasn't nothing to me," she said.

August didn't reply to that but did look as if he was a little rattled. She wouldn't blame him if he was. She was an interloper on the course and had single-handedly become a walking danger zone.

Betsy was rattled too, but it didn't have as much to do with wayward golf balls as it did with her heart. August was starting to make her think about things that she'd given up on ever happening. Things like romance and courting.

It made no sense. She was only in Florida

for a month and barely even knew August Troyer. She needed to stop being so silly and stop thinking about things that could never happen.

Unfortunately, that didn't seem possible.

8

August took Betsy to a cute sandwich shop named Surf City Subs, and she loved everything about it. The restaurant was a small wooden building painted a bright turquoise blue and situated on the edge of Pinecraft. It was kitschy and adorable. Inside there was only room for a counter, the sub's kitchen, and a dining area that barely fit three wooden tables.

There was also a window outside where customers could walk up to the counter and order, and a delightful area with about a dozen tables, half under a bright yellow awning and the other half in the sun.

August led her to the walk-up window. After they'd ordered two turkey subs, drinks, and chips, he insisted on paying. Then they chose a table under the awning while they waited for their order to arrive.

"This place is so cute." Noticing that there was only one other Amish person there,

Betsy added, "I guess you know about a lot of spots that aren't the usual go-to Amish places."

August nodded. "I love Yoder's, but at least half of the diners there are tourists. There's always long lines and people are chatty. Sometimes I just want to eat a sandwich and relax, you know?" He raised a hand when a server came with their order a few minutes later. "Danke," he said.

Suddenly starving, Betsy unwrapped her sandwich and took a bite. "This is so good."

August smiled. "I'm glad you like it. I think they have some of the best sandwiches around. They use really fresh meat and cheese."

"I'll have to see if Mary and Jayson have been here before. If not, I'll have someplace to take them."

"Mary is your good friend and Jayson is her husband, right?" he asked before he took another bite.

"Right. About a year ago, Mary, Lilly, and I all met on a Pioneer Trails bus. We got stuck in an ice storm and ended up having to share a motel room together in Georgia."

He whistled low. "Wow. I bet that was scary."

Smiling at the memory, she nodded. "At first it really was. It was the first time any of

81

us had traveled away from home by our-selves, and we were all so nervous. But within a few hours, our 'worst night ever' became just about the best night ever. We told stories and laughed and ate pizza until the early hours of the morning. By the next day, the three of us were best friends."

His eyes lit up. "And you still are?"

"We still are." Whenever Betsy thought about how the Lord had blessed them with each other at just the right time in their lives, she got choked up. "Until I met Mary and Lilly, I had thought I was the only girl who was a wallflower."

"A wallflower?"

"You know, a girl who doesn't quite fit in. She stands in the shadows and goes un-noticed by just about everyone."

August's expression turned soft. "Betsy, I'm sorry, but I can't imagine that. You light up a room."

His words were so sweet and caught her so off guard that she struggled again. "Ah . . . thank you." She bit her lip then added, "I-I had a far worse stutter when I was growing up. It still comes back when-ever I get nervous. I got made fun of a lot."

"I'm sorry about that."

"M-me too, but, um, it's all in the past."

"And now you're staying with Mary for a

whole month and knocking out a list of things you want to do?"

"Yes."

His voice softened. "Why do you have a list, Betsy?"

She shifted uncomfortably. "It's kind of a long story."

He took another bite of his sandwich, obviously ready for her to tell him all about it.

But still Betsy hesitated. What if she told him everything and he became yet another person who was looking at her like she was fragile? Or, worse . . . what if he thought she was strange because not only did she want to play golf but she also wanted to learn to swim, ride a bike . . . catch a fish?

What kind of woman her age wanted to do any of that? Most were focused on getting married and having children.

She sipped her Arnold Palmer and wondered just how much to share.

He crumpled up the sheet of waxed paper that had been around his sandwich. "Hey, sorry."

"What?"

"You don't need to share anything more. It's obvious that it's personal and none of my business."

"No, there's nothing for you to apologize

for. It's not that personal, I'm, um, just wondering how much to tell you." She looked down at her half-eaten sub. "You're probably going to think I'm even stranger than you already do."

"I haven't thought you're strange at all."

"No?"

He shook his head. "No." A wrinkle formed on his brow. "Betsy, I grew up as a mission kid. My parents are missionaries and carted me all over the world while they tried to make a difference in people's lives."

"That's . . . that's really commendable."

"It is, but it wasn't always easy for a kid, you know? I was always new, always different, and always told not to complain." The shadows lurking in his eyes told her that there was a lot to his story that he wasn't sharing.

"I guess I'm not the only one at this table who experienced some challenges, am I?" she said.

"I've decided that every person in the world has his or her own struggles. All I'm saying is that I'm not going to put you down, Betsy. Not for things you know how to do . . . or for things you don't. I mean, you didn't really imagine that I would look down on you because you didn't know how to play golf, did you?"

"Of course not. I mean, I know that lots of Amish women don't know how to play golf."

"But?"

"But . . ." She paused, then changed her mind. What did it matter if he thought she was strange or not? "You know what? I'm being silly. The short version is that I was in the hospital with a bad case of croup when I was little, and it made my mother scared. I've had pneumonia a time or two as well. Because of all that, I didn't get to do a lot of things that might cause me to have trouble breathing. Now I'm trying to make up for lost time."

"But you're okay now?" His gray eyes were warm and filled with concern.

She smiled at him. "Very much so."

"What's on your list? I mean, will you share a few things?"

"I'm happy to share some of my list, but you have to promise not to laugh."

"I'm not going to laugh. At least not too much."

Betsy took another bite of her sandwich to give herself some time to think about what to say.

But then she realized she'd been looking at everything all wrong. His quip was a good reality check. Her life list was all about hav-

ing fun and experiencing new things —
things that she might never be any good at
or even enjoy. All that mattered to her was
that she tried something new and took some
chances.

If that was the case, then why was she so
determined to make sure that he took
everything so seriously?

"You can laugh all you want," she replied.
"Just, you know, don't laugh too loud."

"I'll be sure to contain myself." His eyes
were bright with mischief.

She pushed the last of her sandwich aside.
"Okay, here we go . . . learning to play golf
and actually playing a whole round is on
my list. And so is fishing."

"Fishing? For what?"

"Ah, fish?"

His lips twitched. "Deep sea fishing? Toss-
ing a line in a pond? Catch and release?"

"I haven't thought that far, I guess. All
I've been thinking about was baiting a hook
and working a rod and reel."

"Okay . . . what else?"

"Well, last time I was here I rode a three-
wheeler bike for the first time. I want to go
riding again . . . and maybe even conquer a
real bike."

"Real bike. Got it." He smiled. "Next?"

Feeling emotionally naked, Betsy reminded herself that she wasn't supposed to be feeling awkward — or care if August was attempting not to laugh. "I think the last big thing on my list is swimming."

"You want to swim in the ocean?"

"No. I want to learn to swim and then swim in a pool . . . and maybe one day not be afraid to go in the ocean."

"That's a lot to accomplish in one month."

"I think so too. Whenever I dwell on my list for a long time, I feel overwhelmed."

"You should be proud of yourself, Betsy."

He sounded so sincere that she felt embarrassed. After all, her dreams weren't important ones. Just wishes about things she wanted to do one day. "For what? Dreaming of learning to do a bunch of things that most people are able to do before they're seven or eight?"

He frowned. "Hey, don't do that. Don't put yourself — or your dreams — down. It doesn't matter when or if you want to do these things. What matters is that you want to push yourself to learn something new. Ain't so?"

"I want to believe that," she admitted. "But sometimes, if I'm being honest with myself, I feel like all I'm doing is attempting to make myself feel better about things that don't really matter." As hard as it was to keep sharing her thoughts, Betsy continued. August was actually listening to her instead of pushing off her ideas as childish or cautioning her to be careful. "My mother even hinted before I boarded the bus that I should be spending a lot more time pursuing a relationship with someone close to home."

He smiled slightly. "She wants you to go on a husband hunt?"

She shrugged. "She wants me to be happy and secure, and the best road to those things — from her point of view — is that I find a good man to take care of me."

It was obvious that August was trying not to laugh. "I see."

"I don't exactly blame her. I mean, I know her heart is in the right place. It's just that even if I did fall in love and get married, I would still feel this nagging need to do these things." She gazed into his gray eyes. "I mean, why can't I learn to swim and play golf and fall in love at the same time?"

"I don't think there's any reason at all that you couldn't do that."

She smiled. "I'm sorry. I guess you can tell this is pretty important to me."

"It should be. It's your life. If it would make you feel any better about your list, I can tell you that a lot of people never play golf or fish or ride bikes or swim. A lot of people don't do a lot of things that others take for granted."

"I guess you're right."

"Why don't you think of everything in a different way? Think of how many people never want to do anything new. Who don't even appreciate someone else's experiences? There's plenty of people like that too."

"Thanks for the pep talk. I'm going to try to stop being so embarrassed and start feeling prouder about what I'm trying to do."

"Gut. Because I'm going to be real proud of the fact that I've helped you."

He was so easy to talk to. Not only that, he was taking her list seriously instead of discounting it. Betsy felt like hugging him. "Thank you for listening. You've given me a lot of good advice."

"Anytime, Betsy. Anytime at all." His smile was so warm and his words were so sincere she could hardly look away.

9

Standing in line at Surf City Subs, Annie couldn't help but overhear Betsy's animated conversation. She'd noticed the young woman from the moment she'd stood in line and had been glancing over at her, waiting for the opportunity to say hello.

It soon became obvious, however, that Betsy had a lot more on her mind besides saying hello to the woman she met on the SCAT. She didn't mean to eavesdrop, but as Betsy got more emotional, her voice carried a little bit more.

Annie couldn't seem to stop listening. Not only did she believe that a lot of women felt they'd been wallflowers growing up, but she agreed with the young man's statement that everyone had some kind of problem in their past to get through.

But what resonated the most for Annie was Betsy's list of activities. She loved the idea of it. Her heart went out to her as she

heard how sad the girl was about not knowing how to do some of those things. All
children liked to fit in. Annie could imagine
how Betsy felt.

At least the girl had found a good friend
in that young man. His speech made her
want to start clapping. Annie noticed that
Betsy was very moved by his words as well.
She might be mistaken, but she was pretty
sure that Betsy was falling head over heels
for that guy — and who could blame her?

"Here's your number," the woman behind
the counter said, catching Annie's attention.
"Put it on your table, and someone will
bring your food out to you."

"Thank you." She walked by Betsy's table.
Since there was a lull in their conversation,
Annie decided to go ahead and stop. "Hi,
Betsy. I just wanted to say hello. We met on
the bus to Siesta Key the other day."

Betsy looked up in surprise, then smiled.
"Your name is Annie, right?"

"Right."

"August, this is Annie. She's visiting
Sarasota as well."

"It's good to meet you." He stood up and
held out his hand. "I'm August Troyer."

"Annie Jackson." She smiled. "Well, you
two enjoy your lunch." She walked to a table
in the corner, dutifully attached her number

to where she was supposed to, then sat down to wait.

Soon after Annie's food came, August told Betsy goodbye and walked away. Betsy glanced in her direction.

"Did you get a turkey sub too?"

"No. It's the veggie one. I'm always trying to eat more vegetables."

Betsy grinned. "Is it good?"

"It's delicious. Everything on the menu looked good. Do you come here a lot? I would."

"It's the first time I visited here." Looking uncomfortable, Betsy added, "I guess it fits in with my goal for this trip, which is to try a lot of new things."

Here was her opening. "Would you like to sit with me for a moment? I overheard something you said — and I might be able to help you with something."

Looking wary, Betsy moved to her table but didn't sit down. "What did you hear me say?" Before Annie had a chance to reply, she pressed a palm over her mouth. "Oh no. Did you hear me talking about my list?"

"I did." When Betsy looked both embarrassed and irritated that Annie had been eavesdropping, Annie added quickly, "Please, just give me a moment. I'm not trying to be rude. I promise."

"All right." She sat down on the edge of her seat. At first glance, one might even think that she was sitting like a proper Amish young lady. But Annie could see the slight pinch in her expression. It was obvious that she was joining Annie very reluctantly.

"Betsy, I'm staying with my sister, and she has a private swimming pool. And she and I both used to be on a swim team together. In addition, I used to lifeguard and Danielle used to teach swimming lessons. I don't know if you're already planning to take lessons somewhere, but if not, Danielle and I could help you learn to swim."

Betsy's eyes widened. "Are you serious?"

"Of course I am. I wouldn't have mentioned it if I wasn't."

"That is so nice of you."

"You don't have to take me up on my idea. I . . . well, I think learning to do new things as an adult can be hard. Kids don't mind failing or messing up, but adults usually don't do that so well."

"I didn't want to learn in the ocean," Betsy admitted. "The currents and the fish scare me."

"I don't blame you. Though the saltwater makes it easier to float, the pool is a much safer environment."

"I appreciate your offer. It was kind of you to mention it."

"I'm happy to help." She pulled out her purse and wrote down her name and phone number on a piece of paper. "If you decide to take me up on the lessons, give me a call." She softened her voice. "And, if you choose not to call, I'll understand."

Betsy took the slip of paper and examined it. "Your sister won't mind?"

"I'm sure she'd be delighted to help you. Danielle can't work on her tan all the time, you know."

Betsy smiled. "I guess not."

"Would you like anything more to drink, ladies?" a cute girl dressed in a long, printed dress asked.

"I'm good," Betsy said.

"I am too," Annie said. "Thank you, though."

"Enjoy your meal," the server chirped before moving on to the next table.

Looking back at Annie's plate, Betsy stood up. "I'm going to let you eat now. Plus, I've got to get back to my friend's house."

"Have a good afternoon."

"Jah. You too."

As Annie watched her walk away, she wondered if Betsy would ever take her up on the offer. Annie figured there was probably a fifty-fifty chance of Betsy calling her.

If Betsy never did, Annie wouldn't blame her. But, as she thought about Danielle, she realized that she hoped Betsy would call. Swimming lessons might do as much good for Danielle and her as it would for that sweet Amish girl.

Two hours later, Annie was pretty sure that she'd been completely delusional. Danielle was staring at her like she'd just asked a criminal to come over to use the pool.

"It was completely inappropriate of you to include me in your conversation."

Honestly, Danielle had never met a situation that she couldn't freak out about.

"Because?"

"Because this is my house, Annie."

"It's your house that you're renting," she corrected. "Plus, you invited me to stay here with you."

"Yes, I did. But I invited you to stay with me. Not take it over and invite people I've never met to come here."

"I think you're making far too much of this. All I'm asking is for you to help someone. I'm sure she wouldn't be here for more than a couple of hours a week." Since Danielle still appeared irritated, Annie added, "That would be at the very most."

"That doesn't matter! Annie, you shouldn't have invited someone to come over without asking me first." One manicured hand slashed through the air. "Worse, you offered my services without even asking. I haven't taught anyone to swim in a really long time."

At last, she got it. Danielle was scared. Finally seeing her sister's point of view, Annie sat down on the lounge chair. "I'm sorry. You're right. I should've asked you first. But — it's not like we don't have extra time."

"I came here to relax. Not teach strangers to swim." She sucked in a breath. "What if she gets hurt? Have you thought about that? What if she gets hurt and she or her family sues us?"

"How can she get hurt? You'll be right beside her, and I would be there in case you need a hand. Plus, we'd be teaching a grown woman how to swim, not do tricks."

"I really haven't taught anyone in years. Decades. And I never taught an adult." She waved her hand again. "And you remember those little guys. They were practically porpoises within two lessons. Adults are much harder."

Annie laughed. "Ah, not all of them." Softening her voice, she said, "Danny, you were a really good swim teacher. You still are an excellent swimmer. I think you've still got it. You'd do fine."

A flash of vulnerability — and maybe pride? — flickered in her eyes before she firmly tamped it down. "We were at the rec center, not a private pool. I had kickboards and noodles."

Annie knew her sister was listing problems . . . but she wasn't saying no. "We could get those things, right?" Before Danielle could protest again, she said, "Just think about it, Danny. I promise, Betsy is such a sweet girl and I think what she's doing is admirable. Plus . . ." She paused, unsure how to describe the feeling she had about the young woman.

"Plus . . . what?"

"Plus, I think she's a little bit like us."

"I don't see how."

"Betsy seems kind of alone right now. I think we might be able to help boost her confidence. Well, you could, since you'd be the main teacher."

Her sister frowned, but it only seemed half-hearted. Like she was thinking that she should be more irritated by Annie's idea than she actually was.

Annie stayed quiet, giving her some time to think it over. She guessed Danielle was weighing the things she was "supposed to be doing" versus what she really did enjoy — which at one time had been swimming in the pool and helping little kids learn to love swimming as much as she did.

After two minutes or so passed, Danielle said, "When did you say this gal was going to call?"

It took everything she had to not smile. "Betsy didn't actually say that she *would* call. I wrote down our names and my cell phone number. She said she was going to think about it. Don't forget, we're strangers to her too."

"Hmm. I suppose that is true." She studied Annie over the rim of her sunglasses. "What do you think she's going to do? Do you think she actually might call? Or do you figure that she's already thrown out your phone number?"

"I think she's kept it. Betsy seems determined to complete this life list of hers. And, since swimming involves a bathing suit and putting her head in the water, I imagine that she's pretty scared. Coming over here for a private lesson would probably make her feel better, don't you think?"

"I do, but you never know, right? I mean, a lot of people say they're going to do things and they never do."

Danielle sounded so bitter, Annie wondered if maybe there was something more that had happened between her and Peter than any of them imagined.

"Hey, Danny?"

"Yes?"

"I don't think you ever told me why you and Peter got a divorce."

Everything in her sister's posture changed. It was like a bolt of lightning had hit her, but instead of it electrifying her, she froze. "Why are you asking me about that? Why now?" Hurt laced her tone.

Making Annie feel guilty. Danielle had a good point. Why was Annie only just now asking about the reasons behind her divorce? Why was she only just now asking about Danielle's side of the story?

Her reasons shamed her. She'd bought into the easy answer. She accepted Peter's explanation and Danielle's silence because they confirmed everything she'd guessed about how her sister had behaved with her husband and family.

But maybe there had been more to the story and Danielle had gotten bitter because it had never occurred to Annie to take her side.

"I'm asking now because I realize I should've asked this a year ago when you and Peter first separated. I'm sorry."

Danielle pulled off her sunglasses. For once she didn't have on a full face of makeup. Devoid of her usual dark brown eyeliner and thick black mascara, her eyes looked haunted and tired.

"I'm not going to lie, Annie. There were many days when I would have given a lot for you to ask me that. But now?" She chuckled bitterly. "Now it feels far too late."

"Why too late?"

"Because talking about my marriage or what happened isn't going to change anything. What's done is done, right?"

Annie swallowed the lump in her throat. "I'm sorry. I should've tried harder to talk to you. I guess . . . I guess I didn't want to pry." Her words felt empty, though. Hadn't she been more interested in taking care of herself? Hadn't it been more of a case of her wanting to avoid Danielle and her bitterness?

"It doesn't matter. As far as the world is concerned, Peter was a saint to put up with me for this long." She shrugged. "Maybe the world is right. I'm not easy."

"You're right, but no one is perfect. I'm certainly not asking you to be. I'm sorry if I made you feel alone."

Danielle didn't say anything for a moment. But maybe she didn't need to? Her expression was so filled with pain and regret that words would seem superfluous. Finally, she slipped her sunglasses back on and stood up. "Annie, if this Amish girl does call, I'll go ahead and help her learn to swim. But I'm going to do it for her — not because you obviously feel like I need some purpose or a project in my life."

"Danielle, it wasn't like that." Though, it kind of had been, now that she thought about it. Remorse filled her.

"I think it was. So, if it's all the same to you, don't do this again. And, just so you know, if you're staying here out of pity or because my children want to hear how I'm doing without actually bothering to call me to find out, I'd rather you go ahead and leave. I might be lonely, but I'm used to being alone. Some might say I'm good at it."

"I really am sorry."

"Don't worry about it." She paused at the sliding glass door. "That's one thing I learned to do real well while living with Peter."

Feeling like the bottom had fallen out of their discussion and she was free-falling, Annie stared after her sister. What had just happened?

And why did she feel like she'd made

everything a whole lot worse instead of better . . . for both of them?

10

Betsy took her time walking back to Mary's house. She needed a minute to wrap her head around the surprising morning — she couldn't seem to stop thinking about what all had happened and been said.

Or that she had seriously underestimated what this project she'd instigated would be like.

When she'd first dreamed up her life list, she'd had no expectations beyond getting out of her comfort zone a bit. It seemed God had other plans, however. First He had placed a number of people in her life who seemed only too happy to help her achieve her goals. Then, He'd been encouraging her to think bigger. Now Betsy wasn't only thinking about checking things off her list, but she was also imagining what her life could be like in the future.

She was starting to realize that her expectation of returning to her quiet, closely supervised life in Kentucky was foolish. And impossible.

The fact was that she was already changing. No longer was she going to be okay with her mother constantly hovering over her every move. Unfortunately, she had no idea what she was going to do about that.

When she walked into her friend's kitchen, she noticed that Mary was in the middle of making a pie. She was standing at the sink washing strawberries. Content to watch her for a moment, Betsy reminded herself that her girlfriend had once been just as confused as she was.

Mary turned off the faucet, turned, and then practically jumped a foot. "Betsy! You startled me."

"I'm sorry. I didn't want to bother you while you were busy."

"While I was washing strawberries?"

It was a stupid excuse. She shrugged. "Okay, I guess it was more like I needed a moment."

Stepping closer, Mary scanned her face. "Are you all right? Did the heat get to you this morning or something? Do you want a glass of water?"

"Not at all. I'm fine. I just was standing here thinking about all my news to tell you."

Mary's expression eased. "I can't wait to

hear about it. Come sit down and tell me everything while I finish this pie."

"I'd rather help. What can I do?" she asked.

"You can slice the strawberries if you'd like so I can press the cookie crust in the pan."

"I've never eaten this kind of crust. It sounds so good."

"I hope it will be. I haven't made it in a few months, but it sounded good today. Plus, Yoder's Market had some beautiful berries on display. They were practically calling out to me to make a pie."

Betsy washed her hands, then picked up the knife and started hulling and slicing berries. "Did you grow up cooking a lot? I did."

"You know, I kind of didn't. I always wanted to draw or paint or sew or even clean. Then, when my little card-making business took off, I had an excuse not to help too much in the kitchen. It was only a couple of years ago that I decided to help my mother more." She smiled. "Of course, when I got engaged, I flew into a panic, thinking that Jayson was going to expect all kinds of gourmet meals when we got married."

"You're smirking. Does that mean he didn't expect those things?"

Mary chuckled as she put the pie crust into the oven and set the timer. "He didn't at all. Not even a little bit. Jayson told me that he likes my cards and artwork — and admires that I've made a success of my business. He doesn't want me to work all day cooking, cleaning, and doing laundry."

"That's a relief."

"It was." Curving one of her hands around her middle, she murmured, "I have a feeling after the baby comes, I'm going to want to do all of those things. Right now, though, I'm just trying to find a good balance."

"I'm happy to take over the meals while I'm here. You'll have more time to draw."

"Danke, but I like being in the kitchen. I can't make many things yet, but I'm learning. Besides, Jayson cooks a lot already."

"He does?"

"Jayson's a pretty good cook. He cooks two nights a week, one night we have leftovers, one night we go out to eat, and then the other three involve my cooking — which is sometimes soup and sandwiches, and sometimes I try my hand at making a roast chicken or a casserole or something."

"I can help you make some casseroles or at least give you recipes."

"Danke." She exhaled. "Enough about me. I want to hear about your lesson — and what you've been doing since then. Your lesson was only an hour, right?"

Betsy felt her cheeks flush. Here she was, offering all kinds of help — but she'd been gone half the day without a word or an explanation. "I'm sorry. I should've been more considerate."

Mary shook her head as she sprinkled sugar on top of the strawberries and stirred them. "Betsy, Jayson and I meant what we said when you first got here. We want you to feel comfortable and use the house as a home base. Beyond, oh, asking you to be careful and such, I'm not going to keep tabs on you."

"In that case, my golf lesson was scary and fun and aggravating and exciting."

"At least it wasn't boring, huh?"

"It wasn't that at all." Thinking of how close she'd stood to August and the way he'd touched her hands when he'd adjusted her grip, she added, "August was patient with me, especially since I learned that hitting a little white ball with an iron club isn't all that easy."

"It's never looked very easy to me." Mary wrinkled her nose. "Or very fun, if I'm being honest." Grabbing Betsy's hand, she added, "Come sit down. The pie crust has ten more minutes and then it has to cool before I put the strawberries in." After they sat down, she asked, "So, were you ever able to hit it?"

"I did! Well, I hit a golf ball pretty good at the end. Then August suggested we go to the sub shop and have a sandwich together."

"Hmm."

"What?"

"Why did he want to take you to lunch?"

She wasn't exactly sure, though she knew how she felt about being with him. "I think he was just being nice."

"Oh? Does he take all his students out to lunch after their lessons?"

"He doesn't." She couldn't help but smile since she knew she was his only golf student. "He's really easy to be around, Mary."

Mary's expression turned knowing. "You like him, don't you?"

"I shouldn't."

"But you do. Ain't so?"

There was no reason to deny it. "Even though I shouldn't like August so much, I do. He's so different from any man I ever met, Mary. He's confident but not all stuffy. He's Amish but not sheltered. And, he seems to know things."

"Know things? What do you mean?"

"I mean that August told me that he grew up all over the world since his parents are

108

missionaries. I think that made him a little bit more sophisticated than most men."

A line formed between Mary's eyes. "Is that a good thing?"

"I think so. It's like catnip to me, Mary. Here all I want to do is try new things, and that has been August's whole life."

Looking more concerned, Mary said, "What are you two going to do if things get serious?"

"It won't get serious."

"But what if it does?"

Betsy shrugged. "I don't have that answer." Not wanting to dwell on that, she moved on to the next part of her lunch and relayed to Mary about how she shared her list with August — and how Annie had overheard and offered her swimming lessons.

Mary's eyes were wide. "Betsy, who would've thought?"

"I know! It feels like God has decided to give me His full attention today. There could be no other explanation for Annie's generosity."

"What did you say? Did you accept?"

"Nee. Accepting her invitation right away felt strange. It's one thing to think about learning to swim, it's a whole other thing to do something about it."

"With a woman you hardly know."

"Exactly. I'm not ruling it out, though. Annie gave me her phone number so I could think about it."

"That's a lot to think about."

Betsy nodded. "I'm a little stunned about how fast everything is happening. After so many years of simply wishing for some opportunities, now it's like I can't stop them from popping up. Part of me wants to get on my knees and tell the Lord that while I appreciate His attention, maybe I don't need to do everything quite so fast."

Mary's lips twitched. "I don't know, Betsy. You do only have a month, and there's a good chance that it's going to fly by."

"So you think I should accept Annie's offer?"

"I think you should think about it. But maybe let me or even Esther go with you, so you're not at their house by yourself."

Esther was another friend she'd made last year. "Maybe." While it might make Betsy feel safer, taking one of her friends along didn't seem right, either. Betsy wanted to do these things on her own. "Maybe I'll ask one of you . . . if I decide to take Annie up on her offer."

"Think and pray on it, Betsy. That's all you can do, right?"

"Right." Hearing the timer, Betsy stood up. "I'll go get the pie shell out of the oven and then I'm going to do a little bit of laundry for you. Is all of your laundry in the laundry room?"

"Jah, but you don't need to do —"

"I want to," she said with a smile as she hurried to turn off the timer. "Rest and then maybe we can get out of the house together for a little bit later."

"Sounds good. Danke."

As she took the pie plate out of the oven, Betsy chuckled to herself. In the other room, Mary was attempting to stifle a loud yawn. No doubt Betsy would discover her asleep on the couch on the lanai within minutes.

That would work well for her because then she could have plenty of time to think about her list, Annie's offer, and the way August Troyer had looked at her when they were on the driving range.

Almost as if no one else in the world existed.

No, almost if no one else in the world mattered.

What was hard to admit — even just to herself — was that she had been likely looking at him in the same way. She hoped he hadn't noticed, or if he had, that she hadn't just embarrassed both of them. Especially because she didn't know hardly anything about his family or his life.

Or if he was already courting someone.

Feeling even more flustered, she hurried to the laundry room, which was nice and bright, thanks to the large picture window over the stationary tub. She began to sort clothes and sheets and towels.

"Think about now," she whispered to herself. "And count your blessings instead of wondering what else is going to make you happy."

That, she decided, was what she would do her best to do for the rest of the day.

There was likely no better use of her time.

11

Several days after Betsy's first golf lesson, August and Nate were on a bike ride. After first cruising along the scenic trails around the nature preserve, they headed over to Pinecraft Park. It wasn't very crowded, and it was late enough in the day that the worst of the sun's beating rays had eased. They both had the day off work and were outside enjoying the beautiful day.

August figured that the two of them should be having a great time. Unfortunately, they weren't — mainly because Nate seemed determined to let him know just how unhappy he was.

"When did you say we could stop?" Nate called out over his shoulder.

August rolled his eyes. "I didn't mention a time. All I said was that I wanted to ride for a spell before we went out to eat at Yoder's."

"Have you ridden long enough yet?"

"I don't know."

"All right. Then how about this question. When can we head over to Yoder's? It's really hot out, you know."

He knew. He also knew that Nate could play eighteen holes on hotter days — and barely break a sweat. "How about we go in ten minutes?"

Nate sighed. "Fine, though I still have no idea why you wanted to go on a bike ride in the first place. We're not teenaged boys, you know."

"Believe me, I know. Relax and pedal. Or go park in the shade and wait for me. I don't care."

"Gut. I'll be over in the covered area. Come get me whenever you're ready to stop sweating."

August didn't give him the benefit of a reply. He just kept pedaling. And, of course, thinking about Betsy. He hadn't told Nate, but she was the main reason he'd suggested the bike ride in the first place. Ever since she'd shared her list, it had been hard for him to think of anything else.

The truth was that he found her list intriguing. It made him think about his childhood and all the things he'd never done when he'd been living overseas. There were quite a few things too. He hadn't missed them when he'd been small — but that was mainly because he hadn't known any kids who had gone roller skating or bike riding or snuck out of the house to watch videos during their rumspringa.

It was only when he got back to America and started making friends like Nate that August had felt the loss of all those rites of passage. He'd wondered what he'd been missing — and if he'd actually been missing out or if he was simply looking for something to be upset about.

Somehow Betsy's list and his need to help her had melded in his head that afternoon. When he'd spied Nate on the golf course, he'd asked if he wanted to ride bikes to the park and then head over to Yoder's for supper.

Nate had been skeptical but had agreed to go. But all it had taken was fifteen minutes in the hot summer sun for him to start complaining.

For the most part, August didn't blame him. It was over ninety degrees, and the humidity matched the soaring temperatures. The air was so thick, it was like they were riding bikes in the middle of a sauna. Though it didn't bother him all that much — he was used to working outside in the heat — he reckoned there was a reason they didn't see a whole lot of people at the park. Everyone else was either at the beach or inside.

After making another loop around the area and deciding that it would be a perfect place to teach Betsy how to ride a two-wheeler bike, he headed over to his friend.

Nate had moved to sit under a palm tree. His eyes were closed.

"Hey, you ready?"

His head popped up. "I am if you are."

"I'm ready. Let's go."

They biked out of the park and down Beneva. Luckily there was a bike lane and they were able to ride easily to the back entrance of Yoder's where the bike racks were.

They were seated without having to wait in line and given drinks right away. And after downing half a glass of iced tea, Nate looked like his regular self again.

"Want to tell me the real reason why you decided to go bike riding in June?" he asked after they put in their orders to the server.

"You know how I sometimes like to do stuff I didn't do as a kid."

"I do know. And I do get it . . . but I don't think you've been missing out on summer bike riding in Florida. What's the real reason?"

"It has to do with Betsy," he admitted.

Nate's eyebrows rose. "Your golfing student?"

"Jah." He laughed. "We had lunch together after her first lesson and she told me about her life list. I can't seem to stop thinking about it."

"A life list?" He frowned. "What's that?"

"It's a list of things she wants to do now. One of them is to learn to play golf and another is to learn how to ride a two-wheeled bike." Thinking of how earnest she'd been, he waved a hand. "She's got a whole slew of things she's anxious to try."

"She doesn't know how to ride a bike? Are you sure she's Amish?" he joked.

Even though his buddy was teasing, August figured he had a good point. Though there were some communities that didn't allow their members to ride bikes, most did. Since the Amish didn't drive vehicles, almost everyone rode a bike from an early age. It was far easier to pedal a bike than to hitch up a horse and buggy.

August nodded. "It took me off guard too. I feel sorry for her. She's wanting to do a lot of things that most people take for granted."

"Why didn't she learn?" He lowered his voice. "Was her family that bad off?"

"I don't think it was because they couldn't

afford a bike."

Nate leaned back against the booth. "That would be hard to believe. I grew up in Charm, Ohio. I know if there had been some kinner in our church district who needed bicycles, the other families would've taken care of that for them. Why, my grandfather spent all of his extra time repairing bicycles and fixing ones up that he found at resale shops and such."

"It's true, though. There's no reason for her to lie about it."

"Jah. I guess you're right."

August shrugged. "I don't really care about why she didn't learn to do some things. I just want to help her out."

"That makes sense." Nate seemed preoccupied as their server, a pretty blond Amish girl, placed two plates in front of them.

"Here you go. One club sandwich plate and one fried chicken salad plate. Anything else?"

"More tea, please, Brianna?" Nate asked.

The server smiled at him. "Of course. I'll be right back."

Popping a potato chip in his mouth, August smiled at Nate's entree. "You get a salad every time we're here."

"I like salads." He speared a piece of

118

ranch-covered romaine. "They're good for you, you know."

"I know." He wasn't sure how much better a fried chicken salad was for a person than his club sandwich, but August supposed it didn't matter.

"You know what? I like the idea of having a life list. Maybe I should do one of those too."

"Really? What would you put on it?"

Nate put down his fork. "If I tell you, you can't tell anyone else."

"I won't. What is it?"

He swallowed. "Well, you see . . . I've never gotten up the nerve to go courting."

August just about choked on his drink. "Nate, you flirt with all the girls."

"I know I do. It's fun. They flirt back. That's fun too." He took a deep breath. "It's never serious, though. I've never taken it a step further. You know, gone up to the door, knocked, and come calling." He visibly shuddered. "Just the thought of that makes me queasy."

"Why?"

"What if I come calling and the girl turns me away at the door?"

"I don't think that ever happens."

"It might. In any case, that's on my life list." Looking more determined, Nate said,

"I want to finally gather up my courage and go calling."

"You want to sit in a woman's parlor and eat cookies and sip lemonade while her mother hovers nearby?" He knew he sounded incredulous, but that was because he was. Nate was the last man he knew who would want to subject himself to the whole awkward event.

"I do. And don't you start laughing, neither," Nate added, looking rather hurt. "I'm being serious."

"I get that. I just don't understand why you want to do such a thing."

"It's a rite of passage, don't you think?"

August had to think about that one. "I suppose so."

"Have you gone courting? Have you done the whole lemonade, cookie, mother hovering thing?"

"I did. Soon after I moved here, I paid a call on Katie Miller."

Nate grinned. "You called on Katie? Did she even let you inside?" He popped a piece of chicken in his mouth.

Katie used to have the reputation of being particularly hard to please. He'd soon learned that her reputation had come naturally. "This was several years ago, you know."

"I figured that, since she's married and all now. I heard she's expecting her first babe."

Leave it to Nate to point that out. "Anyway, what I'm trying to tell ya is that I went calling on Katie, and it was one of the most awkward hours of my life. She kept staring at me like I was going to do something odd, her mother kept acting like I was going to try and kiss Katie, and the cookies were stale."

Nate grinned. "You cared about what the cookies were like?"

"Well, jah. I grew up in missions. Not a lot of folks are making chocolate chip cookies in the middle of Africa."

"I guess not, but I still think it's an odd thing to care about."

"It was memorable."

"Please tell me your other courting visits went better."

"They did. But I've only called on two other women. Both went fine and no one hovered."

"But you didn't get serious with them, did you?" A wrinkle formed in the middle of Nate's brow. "Or did you and something happened? We might not have known each other too good back then."

"We didn't know each other real well, but no, nothing ever got serious."

"How were the cookies at the other women's houses?"

August laughed. "The cookies were great." After eating another bite of his sandwich, he said, "Since you now know my entire courting history, any chance you want to tell me who you intend to call on?"

Nate's expression shuttered. "What makes you think that I have a specific woman in mind?"

As much as August didn't want to put him on the spot, he couldn't ignore the obvious. "Because you're twenty-five years old and no man your age is going to subject himself to the awkward courting dance just for fun?"

Nate flushed. "I reckon you're right."

"So, who is it?"

"I'd rather not say right now," he mumbled.

August was surprised — and maybe a little bit hurt. He and Nate had been friends for a pretty long time. "Why not?"

"Let's just say that you might be surprised and I'm not in any hurry to explain myself." Looking even more uncomfortable, he added, "Plus, I still have to actually ask the girl. That might take a while."

Figuring that they all deserved their secrets, August nodded. "That's fair. Now, do you want to get pie before we head out?"

Nate raised an eyebrow. "What do you think? I didn't ride around that park for my good health, August."

When the server returned, she said, "Are you two ready for pie?"

"Of course," August replied. "I'll have a slice of coconut cream."

Brianna smiled at Nate. "And you, Nate?"

Nate stared back at her with such a look of longing, she might as well have asked if he wanted a million dollars. "I'll have a piece of key lime, Brianna."

"I'll get that right away, Nate. I mean, I'll get both of those pieces of pie out for you." Twin spots of color formed on her cheeks before she rushed away.

Well, there was his answer! Looking from Brianna to Nate, August whistled low.

Nate looked like he was grinding his teeth. "Don't say a word, August."

August smiled. "I wouldn't dream of it." But he privately thought that Nate had chosen well. Brianna was obviously as smitten with Nate as he was with her. All he probably had to do was summon up the nerve to knock on her door, present himself to her parents, and consume a lot of cookies and lemonade for things to click into place.

Nate was such a good man, it would probably only take one or two visits for Brianna's parents to get used to the idea of having him in their lives.

All told, it seemed a lot easier than anything that might happen between him and Betsy.

Which really was too bad.

12

Nate figured that only he would be dumb enough to ride his blasted bicycle all the way back to the golf course with his best friend because he was too chicken to let August know that he was finally going to make a move. He exhaled in frustration.

He'd known August for years now. August Troyer certainly wasn't the type of person to give him a hard time about asking a girl if he could pay her a formal call. Especially not after they'd just discussed the pros and cons of calling on a girl — stale cookies and all.

But his feelings for Brianna were too important to share with anyone but her. Then, of course, there was the fear in the pit of his stomach that had been festering for the last hour. If she laughed in his face or said she already had a beau, he didn't want August to witness it.

Why in the world had he let Betsy's life

list adventure get into his head?

He was even more sore and sweaty by the time he returned to Yoder's forty minutes after he'd left. He parked his bike in the rack again and climbed off and stretched.

"Weren't you just here, young man?"

He looked over to find an Amish man in his fifties staring at him suspiciously. The man had a long gray beard, a deep tan, and was holding a broom. "Jah."

"What happened? You forget something?"

Yeah. He'd forgotten to finally ask Brianna out! Nate supposed his intention of finally talking to Brianna could be described that way. Not that it was any of this man's business. "I did."

"Lost and found is at the front."

"Danke." He headed up the sidewalk, taking care to look purposeful instead of how he currently felt — like a nervous wreck. Once he was out of the older guy's sight, he paused to take a deep breath. He really needed to get a handle on himself. And wash up. He'd been sweating all day . . . why hadn't he thought about that before he'd pedaled all the way back?

He probably smelled. "You're hopeless, Nate Beachy," he muttered under his breath.

To his surprise, thinking about Betsy's life list calmed him down. She was trying her best to accomplish things that she'd always been scared of or unable to do. If she could do one of those things after the other, he surely ought to be able to approach Brianna and ask her a question.

He could do this.

He entered the restaurant. After first washing his hands, face, and neck in the men's room, he walked right over to the hostess and asked to speak to Brianna.

She was looking at the restaurant's seating chart. "Which Brianna?"

"I don't know her last name. She has blond hair and blue eyes."

She looked up. "Ah. That's Brianna Lapp."

"May I speak to her, please? It won't take long."

But still the hostess didn't move. "Why do you need to speak to her?" Her eyes narrowed. "Was she your server and you had a problem with her?"

"She was our server, but I didn't have a problem."

The hostess raised her eyebrows. "What do you need to see her about, then?"

There were now two couples in line waiting to be seated. All four of them were shamelessly listening.

Nate supposed he couldn't blame them, but he still felt like squirming. Truly, his embarrassment about this task was never-ending.

"It's private."

She folded her arms over her chest. "She's working, you know. She can't go taking breaks every time a boy wants to speak with her."

His stomach sank. "That happens a lot?"

"I didn't say that." Amusement shone in her eyes, just like she was a bored feline and he was the mouse she was toying with.

"So, may I see Brianna Lapp for a moment?" He really hadn't thought this would be so hard.

"Let the boy speak to her, Helen!" a man in what was now a sizable line called out. "It's obvious that he likes the girl."

Helen propped a hand on her hip. "So?"

"So, call her over and start seating us."

"Don't be sticking your nose in my business, Pete."

"I'm trying to get a piece of coconut cream pie before you close. Since you're taking forever, it is my business."

"Pete's got a point," the woman standing just behind Nate said. "Let the boy see the girl and seat the rest of us. We're hungry."

"Fine." Helen pointed to the outside porch. "Go stand out there and I'll get Brianna. Don't you be keeping her long,

128

young man."

"I won't." Since there was every chance that Brianna was likely to tell him no and go back inside, he figured he was telling the truth. Still feeling everyone's eyes on him, Nate strode through the door and moved off to the side.

Stuffing his hands in his pockets, he wondered how long he was going to have to wait.

And then she was there.

Instead of coming through the front door like he'd imagined she would, Brianna appeared from around the back. "Nate?"

"Jah. Hi."

She stopped a few feet away. "Hi." She smiled tentatively before seeming to think the better of it. "I heard you wanted to see me?"

"Yes." He stepped closer. "Brianna, I've been meaning to ask you something for some time now . . . do you have a beau?"

Her blue eyes widened. "Do you mean, like a boyfriend?"

"Jah." He nodded like he needed confirmation. "Is anyone courting you? Do you have someone special already?"

"Why are you asking?"

He exhaled and plunged in. "Because if you don't, I would like your permission to come calling."

"Like at mei haus?"

"Yes." He swallowed.

"Well, um, nee."

His stomach sank. "You don't want me to call?"

Looking amused, Brianna shook her head. "Nee, Nate. I'm answering your first question. I don't have a boyfriend." She smiled softly. "And yes, you may have permission to come calling at my house."

Nate didn't think he could stop smiling if he tried. "That's great. I mean, thank you. What's your address?"

"88 Gardenia Lane." She frowned. "Do you know that street?"

"I've lived here a really long time. I know where Gardenia Lane is." Nate stopped for a minute, gathering his courage. "If I came over one evening soon, will you be there?"

She smiled. "I will after three o'clock."

That was it. She'd given him the green light. He was going courting. "I'll see you then."

She looked adorably flustered. "I'll, um, make some cookies. I know you like half tea and lemonade, but do you like lemonade just on its own?"

Ach, but August was going to have a field day. Knowing she wouldn't understand the source of his amusement, he tried not to laugh. "I do. I like lemonade and cookies very much." Softening his voice, he added, "Danke for letting me pay you a call."

"I'm pleased you asked."

There it was. She'd practically told him she liked him too. "You've made me mighty happy, Brianna Lapp."

Her blue eyes twinkled. "I should get back to work. Helen is kind of a stickler for keeping breaks short."

"I imagine she is." He nodded. "I'll see you tomorrow. Most likely about four o'clock."

Brianna smiled before turning away and hurrying through the front door.

When she was out of sight, Nate leaned against the post. He was a sweaty mess and exhausted. To make matters worse, he now had to ride his bike back home.

"Did she say yes, son?"

He turned to find the speaker. It was the man who'd called out when he'd first arrived. Nate didn't want to guess how the man knew what had happened but reckoned that his visit to Brianna had spread like wildfire through the restaurant. "She did!"

"Good for you. She's a good 'un."

"Let's hope she thinks the same way about me one day," he joked.

"Oh, she'll give ya a run for your money. They all do!" he called out again before walking off.

Ignoring the man's amused cackle — and his sudden worry that maybe Brianna was never going to return his regard — Nate hopped on his bike and finally headed home.

This time, the ride didn't feel so bad. Even though it was still hot and his legs were still sore, none of it seemed to matter anymore.

He had finally done something he'd wanted to do for months . . . and she said yes.

One day he was going to have to tell Betsy how she'd changed his life.

As soon as he survived the first visit.

13

Danielle had her hands on her hips as she surveyed the pool area with a critical expression. "What do you think, Annie? Did I overdo it?"

The patio surrounding the pool looked like it was pulled from a fancy magazine featuring high-end resorts. Bright towels were artfully arranged on lounge chairs. A wide assortment of floats, noodles, and kickboards were laid out on one of the sides of the pool. A large stainless beverage holder was filled with ice, bottles of water, and fitness drinks. A cute melamine bowl held at least a dozen granola bars, bags of pretzels, and bananas. There was also a clear acrylic container filled to the brim with snack mix.

In short, the backyard looked like they were about to receive five or six people for the afternoon.

There was no way Annie was going to tell her sister that, though. Taking care to keep all hints of amusement out of her voice, she said, "Not at all. I think it looks like you care and put some thought and effort into this lesson."

"Oh, good." Danielle chuckled. "If Betsy thinks that, it wouldn't be a lie, would it?"

Annie smiled at her. "Nope."

The truth was that from the moment Betsy had summoned her nerve and called Annie's cell phone, said she wanted to take her up on her offer of swim lessons, and they set a time for noon the next day, Annie and Danielle had flown into a whirlwind of activity.

They made lists of things to get, piled into the car, and headed to the Dollar Store. There they got sunscreen, noodles, kickboards, and two more beach towels. Next, they headed over to the grocery store and got drinks and everything to make "puppy chow," the combination of Chex Mix, nuts, pretzels, and white chocolate.

Danielle had said that they should have something with a little bit of nutrients but a good amount of carbs. But festive. Annie wasn't sure if the puppy chow fit that bill or not — but it sure had been fun to make. She couldn't remember the last time she'd laughed so hard with Danielle. Or made such a mess!

"I hope Betsy likes puppy chow so we can send some home with her," Annie murmured. "I think I've gained three pounds from it already."

"I'd say I did too, except I've been swimming so many laps I feel like I could eat a whole cow and still be just fine."

It was really cute the way Danielle had been intent on being in good shape. She'd been practicing different strokes for the last twenty-four hours.

"How did you say she was going to get here again?"

Annie frowned. "I didn't even think to ask. Maybe she's taking the SCAT?"

"I bet. But maybe one of us could drive her home? I wouldn't mind doing that if you can't."

"I can do it," Annie said. "Now all we have to do is —"

The doorbell rang, interrupting her words.

"She's here! I'll go get her," Annie called out as she hurried to the entryway. To her surprise, Danielle came along. She stayed behind when Annie opened the door.

Betsy was standing on the welcome mat, looking at the house with wide eyes.

"Hi, Betsy," Annie said with a big smile. "I hope you didn't have any trouble getting here? Danielle just reminded me that I could have offered to pick you up."

"I-I took the S-SCAT. So it was no p-problem. I-I'm used to that." She closed her eyes, looking frustrated with herself.

Annie remembered that Betsy had stuttered a little bit. It seemed it got worse when she was nervous. Annie's respect for the girl grew. It was obvious that coming here was out of her comfort zone, plus she was going to learn to swim, which was scary for anyone at any age. "Come on in and I'll introduce you to Danielle."

Still looking hesitant, Betsy picked up a large canvas bag and walked inside. She set it on the tile floor as Danielle clasped her hand.

"I'm Danielle."

"Hi."

Without missing a beat, Danny continued. "I'm so glad to meet you. I think teaching you how to swim is going to be the highlight of my vacation here."

"I sure h-hope not. This house is beautiful."

"Thank you, but it's not ours. We're just renting it for a month." Danielle started walking. "It's got a great pool, though. Come on and I'll show it to you."

After a quick glance at Annie, who gave her an encouraging smile, Betsy picked up

136

her tote and followed Danielle down the hall, past the living room and kitchen, and finally out to the backyard patio and pool.

Annie thought Betsy would be staring at the gorgeous landscaping, or the pool deck, or even the built-in hot tub on the pool's far end. Instead, she was staring at all the items they'd bought at the Dollar Store.

She picked up one of the kickboards. "Y-you two got all this for my lesson, didn't you?"

"We did," Annie said. "But it was no big deal."

"Sure it was. I canna hardly believe you went to so much trouble for me. Oh! I never even asked how much each lesson will be. I'm sorry about that. What do you charge, Danielle?"

Danielle blinked. Looking at Betsy, she said, "I think ten dollars a lesson is fair. What do you think?"

Annie was shocked and horrified. Neither of them had expected to be paid. "Danielle, maybe —"

But then she noticed Betsy stand a little straighter. A bit more confidence appeared in her face too. Annie realized that her sister had been exactly right. Betsy didn't want to be their charity recipient. She wanted to be treated as an equal — which meant that they needed to give her the satisfaction of paying for her lesson. "I think ten dollars is fair. Danke."

"Oh good. Well, now that's taken care of, come sit down and we'll talk about what you want to learn for a moment." The three of them sat down together, and to Annie's amusement, Danielle pulled out a notepad. "I had some ideas, but they aren't set in stone. Take a look and see what you think."

Betsy read the list carefully before looking up at Danielle again. "I-I don't know what kind of strokes I want to learn. I really just want to be able to get in a pool and be able to swim from one end to the other without worrying about drowning. Um, is that all right?"

"I think that's absolutely fine," Annie said. "You're in charge of the lessons, not either of us. We can take things one step at a time."

"I'm not going to let you down, Betsy," Danielle said. "I promise that within two or three lessons you're going to be able to swim."

"Really? Do you think learning to swim is really that easy?"

Looking intent, Danielle leaned toward her. "Not at all. Honestly, I think learning to swim can be really hard to do — but you look like a fighter. Something tells me that you're going to conquer swimming just fine."

The smile that lit up Betsy's face was beautiful. Annie decided right then and there that all the stress and running around had been worth it. Helping someone else was always worth the effort.

Forty minutes later, all three of them were wrapped in towels, sitting around the glass-topped table on the patio, and inhaling puppy chow.

"This is so good," Danielle said. "I haven't had this in forever. Not since we were little girls, Annie."

Picking up another piece, Annie said, "I usually only make it for Christmas. Of course, that means that I give most of it away."

"I've eaten it before, but I can't remember the last time that was," Betsy said. "But I'm pretty sure it was never this good."

Danielle nodded. "I think it's the swimming that makes everything taste better. I used to be starving every time I got out of the pool."

Betsy frowned. "I don't know why I'm so hungry. All I really did was float."

"You did more than that. You got in the water, floated on your back, swam laps using the kickboard, and put your head under water," Annie corrected. "All for the first time."

"You had to be scared half to death, Betsy," Danielle said.

"I think I was more nervous calling Annie than I was when we got in the pool. Today I just kept reminding myself that I was finally doing something that I've been wanting to do for years." She beamed. "I was a little scared but kept wanting to cheer." She covered her mouth. "I bet you ladies think I sound ridiculous."

"I think you sound adorable," Danny replied.

"So . . . how does it compare to golf lessons?" Annie asked.

Immediately Betsy's cheeks turned pink. "It was just as gut."

"Uh-huh."

"It was," Betsy said. "I mean it, Annie."

"I feel like I'm missing something." Danielle looked from one to the other. "What is it?"

"Nothing," Betsy said quickly.

Annie felt guilty for embarrassing her. "She's right. I just happened to notice how cute her golf instructor was. And couldn't help but compare your lessons with a handsome young golf pro to two old ladies."

"You aren't old. And they're two different things."

Danielle laughed. "Betsy, I have to thank you. I don't remember the last time I've enjoyed myself so much. Thank you for letting us help you learn to swim."

"You're welcome."

"Do you want to come back again?"

"I do. Next week?"

"If that's the best time for you, it works for us. Or you could even come back in a couple of days. We're all only here a month, so we might as well get in as many lessons as we can. It's up to you."

"I'd like to come in three days, then."

After they set up the next session, Annie stood up. "I'll drive you home, Betsy. Danielle, do you want to come?"

"Thanks, but I'm going to take a shower. Betsy, I'll see you soon."

"Oh! Here!" Betsy opened up her wallet and pulled out a ten-dollar bill. "Here's your payment. Thanks again, Danielle. You're a good teacher."

Danielle took the money. "You're welcome and I'll see you soon."

"There's a dressing room, Betsy," Annie said. "You get changed and I'll do the same. I'll meet you at the front door when you're ready."

After Betsy darted into the dressing room, Annie walked inside. Danielle was in the kitchen putting away the last of the puppy chow in a big Ziploc bag.

"I was thinking we could send the rest home with Betsy — unless you want it?"

Annie shook her head. "No way. I'd eat the rest tonight."

"I was thinking the same thing."

The smile they shared was so easy and natural, Annie realized that they hadn't exchanged something like that in years.

Which, obviously, was a shame.

She made a promise to herself right then and there that they would fix things between them. It had to get better. It just had to.

14

Nate had told only his mother about his plans to pay a call on Brianna. His father would've had too much to say about what to do, and his brothers and sisters would've first laughed uncontrollably and then teased him about his visit for the next seven years. His siblings were thoughtful like that.

He wouldn't blame his brothers and sisters for teasing him, either. He was the middle child of five and had been unfortunately blessed with the biggest mouth. The other four had grown up listening to him having an opinion about nearly everything. He'd also gone through a phase of tattling. He regretted those few months very much.

So, he wisely kept his plans to himself. He was nervous enough without hearing everyone make jokes at his expense.

Now, though, as he walked the last block to Brianna's house, Nate wished he'd talked to one of his brothers in addition to Mamm.

Either Darren or Mark would have given him some courting pointers after they'd finished teasing him.

Instead, he was simply a mess of nerves. All his mother had said was to make sure he showered and had on a clean shirt. Both of those things were good pointers — except that he had already showered but was now making his clean shirt sweaty.

He was debating whether or not he had time to sit under a nearby tree and cool off when he realized that he was standing in front of the Lapps' house. It was bright white and had black shutters and trim and lovely landscaping. There was also a front porch with a swing and a fluffy cat sprawled out on the railing, its tail lazily swishing back and forth.

Finally, if he wasn't mistaken, he was pretty sure that more than one member of the household was watching him stand in front of their house like an unwanted solicitor.

Rolling his shoulders, he turned and walked to her door. If he wasn't going to be able to get himself together, it was time to start pretending that he was. August was right. He could flirt or chat with just about anyone. He was an extrovert and enjoyed conversation. Surely paying a formal call on

Brianna wouldn't be so hard. All he had to do was try not to think about how much she meant to him.

And how much he could mess up his entire future if he did or said the wrong thing.

With a feeling of dread, Nate knocked twice on the door and prayed for help.

A woman with Brianna's same blond hair and blue eyes opened it. "Hello?"

"Hello. I'm Nate Beachy. I've come here to see Brianna." Inwardly, he winced. Even to his own ears, he sounded like a robot.

A little girl about six years of age peeked out from around the woman's skirt. "I'm Lark."

"It's a pleasure to meet you, Lark," he said to the child. "Is Brianna available?" he added since her mother had still not spoken a word. Or moved to one side.

Lark smiled at him but then hid behind her mother's skirt again.

Nate stuffed his hands in his pockets.

"Where do you live, Nate?" Brianna's mother said at last.

"On the west side. Why?"

"I haven't seen you around very much."

"Oh?" It took him a minute to realize that she was talking about church. "Well, we don't go to the community church. The

145

folks on the three streets near me elected to have church at each other's houses most all the time."

"Ah."

She still didn't move.

Had he said the wrong thing? Had he already made a mistake? "Is, um, Brianna here?"

"Brianna is in her room but will be down here shortly." At last she smiled. "Won't you take a seat on the porch? Brianna will bring lemonade and cookies when she comes out."

Nate hated the idea of her serving him, since she did that at Yoder's all the time. "I could help her carry them."

Her mother looked appalled. "Of course you mustn't do that. You're Brianna's guest. Her sister Tonya will help Brianna if she needs assistance."

Lark popped out from behind her mother. "Tonya is our big sister."

"Ah," Nate said. Feeling like he needed to get himself together, he took a step backward. "I think I'll go sit down."

Lark giggled as she and her mother walked away. Luckily there was a pair of chairs in addition to the porch swing. He quickly sat down and rubbed his hands on his thighs.

Five minutes later, the door opened. Brianna was in a pink dress and holding a white tray with a pitcher of lemonade and three glasses. A woman about one or two years older followed. A platter of sugar cookies with sprinkles was in her hands.

Nate jumped to his feet. "Hello, Brianna."

She smiled and blushed. "Hi, Nate. This is my sister Tonya."

Tonya had the same blue eyes but light brown hair.

"Hi."

Tonya smiled at him. "Hi. I'm going to be acting as chaperone."

Chaperone? Why hadn't August or his mother told him to be prepared for a chaperone? "I see." But of course he didn't "see" at all.

"Having a chaperone wasn't my idea," Brianna said. "I'm really sorry."

"Just so you know, being here wasn't my idea, either," Tonya added. "Our mother is being ridiculous."

"I don't mind if you're here, Tonya," he said quickly. "I mean, Brianna, I'm just glad you allowed me to come over."

Her eyes lit with humor. "Would you like some cookies and lemonade?"

"Yes, please."

"Then sit down and I'll get it for you."

When Brianna turned away, Tonya gestured toward the swing. "Go sit down on the porch swing with Bri," she said under her breath. "Brianna's nervous and I feel like an idiot. We need to make this as easy as possible for her."

He glanced at Brianna again. It was obvious that she'd heard what her sister said and was in full agreement. "Yeah, sure," he said as he sat down on the swing.

Seconds later, he was holding an ice-cold glass of lemonade and a napkin full of cookies.

As the swing moved and rocked, Nate finally understood why August had frowned when he mentioned cookies and lemonade. The problem wasn't so much the quality of the food but whether he could eat and drink without making a fool of himself or choking.

He was currently attempting to drink his lemonade without spilling it, balance cookies on his lap, not slide too close to Brianna, and converse with her about something meaningful while she was doing the same thing.

"This is harder than I thought it would be," he muttered.

"It is?" Brianna looked completely crestfallen.

And . . . things had just gone from bad to worse. "I'm sorry. I didn't mean to say that out loud."

"It's okay." Looking more miserable, she said, "You aren't thinking of anything that I haven't been."

Nate carefully shifted so he could see her face. "Really?"

She nodded. "I don't have much experience with boys coming over. Like, none." She bit her lip. "Worse, I don't know what to say to you, Nate. And that's stupid because whenever I see you at Yoder's, we talk just fine. Whenever you're there, all I want to do is spend more time with you."

"I feel the same way."

Her eyes widened. "Truly?"

"Truly." Raising his voice a bit, he added, "And no offense to Tonya, but I don't know what to say with an audience listening."

Tonya made a dismissive noise. "Nate, I promise, if I could be anywhere else, I would be. Or I'd put earbuds in my ears and listen to music if I thought I could get away with it."

Brianna giggled. "Tonya is 99 percent sure that she wants to go to the community college and become a vet tech. She might become Mennonite so that it's possible."

"Which means you could get earbuds. I hear they're great."

Tonya laughed. "I honestly don't know if

I want them or not . . . but I do think it's silly to chaperone Brianna when she works at Yoder's all day. She can talk to whoever she wants there."

Nate made a decision. He could either keep complaining and wish things were different or he could accept the situation and try to make things better between him and Brianna.

Keeping his voice soft, he said, "Brianna, this is the first time I've ever gone calling on a girl. I promise, all I want to do is get to know you. I think you're really pretty. I like how you always seem to have time for everyone at the restaurant. Even the older men who come inside by themselves and just want to have someone to talk to."

Brianna's expression softened. "Oh, Nate. That's so sweet."

"The truth is that I've been trying to get the nerve to come calling for quite a while."

"Why haven't you?"

"Because I was too afraid you'd tell me no."

Her blue eyes widened. "I wouldn't have told you no."

"I didn't know that, though," he countered. "Be patient with me, okay? This courting thing is new to me, but I want to do it right. I don't want to be disrespectful or make you uncomfortable."

Brianna stared at him for a long moment. Several seconds passed. Then, like the light shining at the end of a long day, she smiled at him. "My favorite color is pink, and I've always wanted a little Pomeranian."

Finally, at long last, everything seemed to click into place. "I've always been partial to green, and I grew up with a chocolate Lab named Trudy who we all adored."

"Do you like Poms?"

"Aren't they fluffy, barky things?"

"Yes."

"Sorry, but no." He chuckled at her stricken expression. "I'm just teasing," he lied. "I promise that if you get a Pom, I'll try to like it."

"Should we say more things we like?"

"Jah." He sipped his lemonade. "I think that's a great idea."

Finally, everything between them settled into place, like one of those games for children where they have to put pegs into the right-shaped holes. Beside him, Brianna relaxed. He did too.

They started talking about her work and his life and siblings and August . . . and then he even told her about Betsy's life list.

When her eyes widened and she declared that she wanted to come up with a list of

her own, Nate knew everything was going
to be okay between them.

15

It was still early — not quite eight in the morning. However, August was already beginning to feel like he'd put in a whole day's work. At least Diane had made a great pot of coffee and a bagel and egg sandwich for breakfast. It was also a blessing that some of his favorite — and longtime — customers had decided to play the course that morning. Catching up with players who had become friends over the last two or three years made the time fly by.

Such as Able Wright. He was a middle-aged Mennonite man with a wicked sense of humor. He also was an amazing golfer. August was pretty sure that Able could hold his own against just about anyone in the private country clubs in the Sarasota-Bradenton area.

"Danke, August," Able said as he took his change and slid the dollars into his wallet.

"You're welcome. It's not too hot. You

should have a good time playing today."

"We will. The word has been going around that the course is looking great right now."

"That's good to hear. I've been trying to make some improvements, especially around holes six and thirteen."

"It's been noticed, son." After peeking to make sure August's aunt and uncle weren't in earshot, he added, "To be honest, I don't think things have ever looked so good."

August smiled to himself. He couldn't deny that it was nice having his hard work appreciated.

"That Able sure had a lot to say," Uncle Gideon said after Able zipped off on one of the gas-powered golf carts.

August turned to him in surprise. "I didn't realize you were here, Uncle."

"Wouldn't make no difference if I was or if I wasn't." He clapped him on the back. "Praise is praise, boy."

"I'm glad the course looks so good. The rain's helped."

"Indeed it has, but the course isn't looking so tip-top because of a couple of rain showers. A lot of the credit goes to you."

"I'm sure Able's praise was for everyone."

"Don't worry, son. I promise, I'm not jealous. As a matter of fact, hearing a compliment headed your way makes me happy.

You're a hard worker. Diane and I couldn't be more proud of the way you've taken on more and more responsibility."

"I'm glad to be here. You didn't have to hire me on."

Gideon slapped him on the back again. "No need to keep being grateful. We know you are. Now all you need to do is figure out if you want to take over the place one day."

"What?"

"You heard me." When August continued to gape, his uncle chuckled. "Come now. I've made no secret of the fact that I don't want to work more than another year or two."

"I didn't realize you were thinking of letting me run the place. I don't know what to say."

"Gut, because there ain't nothing that you need to say."

"How about thank you?"

"How about you say that you'll consider my offer," Gideon countered right back.

"I will." To his embarrassment, August felt his throat get choked up. Growing up, he'd never felt good enough or appreciated by his parents. Now he felt truly honored that his aunt and uncle valued him enough to ask him to run the course they started thirty years ago. "This makes me real happy."

Gideon frowned. "Son, you were a good boy. A fine boy. You've grown into a man anyone would be proud to know. There are moments, however, that I want to march over to whatever continent your parents are on and shake some sense into them. For some reason that Diane and I can never figure out, they never felt the need to make sure you heard those things. I'm sorry about that."

He was too, though it felt ungrateful to actually say the words.

"Ah, someone's arrived at just the right time. Good afternoon, Betsy."

"Hi there, Gideon. How are you today?"

He winked. "Not as good as my nephew here. Enjoy your lesson. Diane's in the back. Ask her to come up front when you leave, August," he said as he walked out the door.

"He sure is nice," Betsy said.

"I think so too. So, are you ready for another lesson?"

"I am, but I think the question should be more if you're ready for another hour by my side at the driving range."

"Of course. I'll go get your golf bag and then we'll be on our way." When he entered the storage room, he noticed his aunt wiping her eyes. "Diane, what's wrong?"

"Nothing. It's just that sometimes I'm so glad I married your uncle. He's a really good man." She hugged him. "What Gideon said about you and your parents is how I feel too. I love my brother, but I never understood the way he took you for granted. I just wanted you to know that. I love you, August."

"I love you too, Diane."

"I'll head up front. You get Betsy's bag and be sure to take her to lunch again."

"Are you sure you don't mind?"

"Very sure. Go have fun."

He picked up the golf bag and carried it out to Betsy. When she made a move to get it, he shook his head. "We're going to load it on a push cart. Come on."

When they reached the corral of carts, he said, "Go grab one of the push carts and wheel it over. I'll show you how to place your golf bag on the cart."

Betsy selected one and rolled it over. "Now what?"

"Pick up your bag and place it on the shelf, faced this way," he said as he pointed to another player's cart. "Then secure it with the belt." Once again, Betsy did as he asked. It took a bit of restraint on his part to simply not place it in position for her, but he was learning the power of giving someone the opportunity to do something for themselves.

When it was all done, Betsy's smile was radiant. "I did it. It wasn't hard at all."

"Next time you come, you'll know what to do."

"I sure will. If I'm ever actually able to hit a golf ball again, I'll be doing great."

He laughed as they walked down the path toward the driving range, Betsy pulling her bag behind her. Today she had on a crisp yellow dress. The sunny color brought out both her dark hair and eyes. She was wearing bright white tennis shoes. They were so white they didn't look like they'd ever been worn. "Did you buy new clothes before you came here?"

She frowned. "I bought a couple of new things, like shoes and a shawl, but I made my dresses. Why?"

It was because he thought she looked so perfect. So fresh and pretty, even when the humidity was high and the temperatures were already hovering in the nineties. "No reason. I was just curious."

"Oh." After walking a few more feet, she blurted, "Do you find that to be vain?"

"Not at all. Forget I asked anything."

It was a slight uphill incline to the driving range. Betsy stayed by his side, but she seemed to be struggling a bit more than she had last time. If he hadn't just asked her about her clothes, August probably would've asked if she was all right. However, he didn't want her to think that he was analyzing everything she did.

He was grateful when she stopped on her own. "I'm sorry. I guess I need a small break."

"Take your time."

She took a few tentative breaths, coughed, then seemed to debate with herself. After another few seconds, she opened up her purse and pulled out an inhaler. "I'm sorry," she mumbled before putting it to her mouth and pressing the top of it. Thirty seconds later, she inhaled another puff and paused.

August could hear her wheezing. It sounded painful and a little bit scary. "Do you need some water? I can go get you something real quick. There are cups at the range."

"Danke, but I'll be all right. I . . . well, I guess I just need a bit more time." She took another few breaths, glanced at the watch on her wrist, breathed again, and then finally put the inhaler away. "I'm sorry about that."

"There's no need to apologize about your health."

She stilled, then smiled at him again. "August, this probably sounds strange, but I don't think you'll ever know how much what you just said means to me."

"Sometimes I think that the Lord gives us the right words to say. Not often, because I've sure put my foot in my mouth a time or two! But every once in a while, He seems inclined to help me out. Maybe that's what He's doing today. I was able to say something that you needed to hear — and I heard something from my uncle that I really needed to hear."

As Betsy started walking again, she smiled at him. "I wouldn't be surprised if He was with us today. So far, it's been a mighty good day."

"I think so too."

Over the next hour it became apparent to August that Betsy had no natural ability for swinging a golf club. He was also beginning to realize that she'd neither practiced nor cared all that much about whether she was improving or not. Over and over again she acted like she was concentrating on her grip, the placement of her elbows, and the movement of her swing and hips. But August had the sneaking suspicion that she was only — for lack of better words — going through the motions.

Instead of acting disappointed when ball after ball popped in the air and then sank like a rock, Betsy smiled and shrugged. And then promptly did the same thing again with the next ball.

August was both charmed and exasperated.

After twenty minutes, he handed her a cup of water. "I think it's time for a break."

"Really? Have we already been playing that long?"

It was comments like that that made him wonder what, exactly, was the purpose for her lessons. Feeling like his future reputation as a golf teacher was at stake, he said, "Betsy, no offense, but do you actually want to become a golfer? I mean, I know learning to play is on your list and such, but do you have any real desire to be able to play a game?"

"Of course. I mean, I'm here, aren't I?"

He noticed she didn't meet his eyes, though. "That is true."

She blinked. "I'm starting to realize that you might be agreeing with me . . . but you're thinking something else. Am I right?"

There was no way he was going to tell Betsy that he was beginning to think that she had no natural ability for golf. So . . . he improvised. "I'm simply thinking that if you really want to learn to swing a golf club but are still having such a difficult time, that I must be doing something wrong. Maybe I should ask someone else to teach you."

"Nee!"

"There's nothing wrong with me admitting that I'm not a gut teacher, Betsy. You won't hurt my feelings."

She put her hand on his forearm. "I don't want another teacher. It's not your fault that I'm not a g-gut g-golfer."

Unable to stop himself, he placed his hand over hers. "Betsy, I'm sorry. I didn't mean to upset you."

"Let's go play putt-putt."

"Pardon me?"

"I'm sorry. I-I mean, let's go to the putting green. I'm sure I'll do better there."

"But —"

She released a ragged sigh. "August, you're right. I don't really want to be a good golfer. In the grand scheme of things, back in Hart County, I'm not going to be heading to the golf course. But this list was never about improving myself."

"What's it about, then?"

"All I really want is to *do* things. I don't care if those silly white balls only go a couple of yards. What I do care about is that I've gotten the chance to give golfing a try.

162

Do you understand the difference?"

"Jah. I finally do." He picked up the 9 iron and put it back in her golf bag. "Let's go to the putting green."

"Are you sure you don't mind?"

"Not at all."

"Will you do me a favor, first?"

"Of course. What?"

"Will you hit a couple of balls with that driver for me? Just so I can see what you look like?"

Hitting balls on the driving range felt a bit like showing off. "I've been playing for several years, Betsy."

"If that's your way of trying to tell me that you can hit a golf ball well, then I should probably let you know that I already guessed that. I still want to see you hit some balls. Now that I've learned how tricky it is, I can appreciate it more."

"Fine." Glancing at the tee next to him, where an Englischer couple in their twenties had been hitting, he made a decision. "Excuse me. May I borrow your driver for a few minutes? She, uh, just wants to see my stroke."

The guy chuckled as he handed August his driver. "No problem."

"Thanks." Feeling a bit foolish, he lined up some balls, did a few practice swings to get the feel of the unfamiliar club, and then reminded himself that Betsy probably couldn't care less how he played.

Feeling his stance ease, he swung back and then promptly hit five balls in a row. Each one sailed through the air, straight and far. If he'd been with Nate, August knew he'd probably be preening, those long drives looked so good.

Instead, he realized he merely felt satisfied.

He walked back to the couple and handed the club over. "Thank you."

"Anytime. You, ah, have a great swing. No wonder you work here."

"Thanks." He smiled and then turned back to Betsy. "Ready to putt now?"

Her eyes were sparkling. "Jah, August. I think I'm ready now."

As he pulled her cart next to her on the path leading to the putting green, August was pretty sure he was having one of the best days of his life. It had nothing to do with the good weather or the condition of the course. Nope, it all had to do with one dark-haired, dark-eyed Amish girl from Kentucky.

16

It was official. Betsy was absolutely, positively, no-doubt-in-her-mind falling in love with August Troyer.

Walking next to him while he pushed her silly golf cart, Betsy felt like she was the most special girl on the whole golf course. Not only was he so handsome but he was very talented. Each one of those golf balls sailed through the air like he never did anything all day but practice.

But neither his looks nor his talent was what made her heart squeeze every time she looked at him. Instead, it was his easygoing manner. Betsy didn't know if August was really humble or if it was more a matter of him not wanting to gloat in front of her. Whatever the reason, Betsy loved that August could be patient with her, hit a bunch of golf balls perfectly with a borrowed club, and then follow her lead when she practically demanded that they go to the putting green.

She could be wrong, but she had a feeling that August would always treat her the way he was treating her now. It seemed like his relaxed manner was the perfect foil for her frenetic pace. He calmed her down . . . and maybe she gave him a bit of needed pep in his life.

When they stopped at the putting green, he pulled out her putter and handed it to her. "Since you're already familiar with putting, given your expertise on the putt-putt course and all, I'm guessing that you already have a good grip. Why don't you show it to me?"

Obviously she shouldn't have acted like she could putt well. "Hmm. Well, come to think of it, I believe it's been a while since I've had a chance to play. Why don't you remind me about the correct putting grip?"

August seemed to be biting his lip in order not to laugh. He didn't argue, though. Instead, he stood behind her and carefully placed her hands on the club. Once again, his touch was careful but firm. Like he knew what he was doing but didn't want to inadvertently bruise her skin.

Unfortunately her mind started to drift toward other ways he could touch her. Ways that she had no business thinking about.

"D-danke. I think I've got it now."

"Am I making you nervous, Betsy?"

"N-nee. I mean, n-not at all." She was so flustered she could barely speak. Her stupid stutter. It was like a truth serum or something.

Immediately he stepped away. She would be lying to herself if she didn't admit that she felt his loss.

He tossed yet another golf ball on the green, this one yellow. "All right, Betsy. Let's see how you do."

Taking a cue from the way he'd allowed himself a moment to get settled in before hitting the driver, she placed her hands on the putter, carefully did two practice swings, eyed the hole, and then tapped the ball.

And . . . it was a thing of beauty. Like a magnet was drawing it toward the flag, the yellow golf ball glided up the incline, around the slight curve, then inexplicably rolled right into the cup.

She'd just got a hole in one!

Even though Betsy had just delivered her very earnest lecture about her need to simply enjoy things without dwelling on success or ability, she couldn't help but grin like a fool as she turned to face him. Finally doing something right in front of August had felt awesome. "So, ah, what do you think?"

He was gaping. No, he looked stunned, shocked . . . and dare she say . . . impressed?

Before she knew what he was about, he picked her up and swung her in a circle. "Betsy Detweiler, look at you!"

The putter dropped to the ground as she laughed and braced her hands on his shoulders. "August, put me down!"

He swung her around again. "No way. That putt was amazing. I've never gotten a hole in one on that stupid putting green. I'm so proud of you. Gut job!" he added as he set her down.

Feeling a little dizzy and a whole lot rattled by just how much she'd loved him twirling her around, Betsy laughed. "You're awfully easy to impress."

"Not hardly. But I am impressed with your putting prowess. I owe you an apology too."

"For what?"

"For being skeptical when you said you could putt. I should've believed you."

"August, you know I was just spouting off, right? I absolutely am not a gifted putter. I just got lucky." She sure couldn't say why the Lord had blessed her with such an achievement!

"Well, it was amazing." His smile was so warm.

All she wanted to do was stare at him . . . and hope that he'd spin her around in his arms again.

"So, um, what should we do now?" she said.

"Now?"

"Well, jah. Don't you remember? Last time I hit a good shot, you suggested we stop on a high note. I think it's obvious that I won't have a better putt this morning. Stopping might be a great idea."

"Hmm. Well, that would mean that we still have some time left for our lesson. I could either take you out on the course and you can play a hole . . ."

"Or?"

"Or we can go for a walk to the nature preserve nearby. There's lots of birds there. Do you like pelicans?"

"I love pelicans!" Okay, she didn't actually *love* them, but there was no way she wanted him to even think for a minute that she didn't want to spend more time with him — without golf clubs in their hands. "Yes, let's go for a walk." She reached for her cart and pulled it behind her, thinking that she could probably follow him anywhere and be happy about it. Thinking about her family, she frowned. Her parents would never let her live far from them. "Hey, August?"

"Yes?"

"Do you ever think about living someplace else?"

"Nee."

That wasn't good. "Never?"

"Never, ever." He glanced her way. "I spent most of my childhood living like a vagabond, you know. I hated it."

"Did you move so much because of the mission work? I'm afraid I have no knowledge about when or why missionaries move around."

"It did have a lot to do with my parents' jobs, but that wasn't the whole reason." Looking straight ahead, he continued. "You see, there are a lot of adults who are missionaries, but they only do the work for a time, then they settle down back at home. Or they ask to stay at their sites for years at a time in order to make connections. They want to stay in one place and bond with the people they're serving. To make a difference, you know?"

When she nodded, he continued. "My parents weren't that way. They were . . . no, they *are* restless. They like to move and try new things. And they like to feel needed."

"I would imagine everyone likes to feel needed."

"I reckon so, but there was more than that going on. They never said no to an opportunity — especially if it was someplace remote or in trouble. It was like they fed off it."

"Oh my."

Still staring ahead, he lowered his voice. "I never knew if I was going to stay in one place for two months or two years."

She heard the pain in his voice — and the fact that he wasn't attempting to hide it from her. "That had to be hard."

His posture eased. "You have no idea how hard it was. Moving around as an adult can be challenging. But for a child, especially an only child, it was near excruciating. You see, it wasn't only about meeting new people and trying to make friends, it was all the other stuff that most kinner take for granted. It was constantly adjusting to new food and new languages. It was being handed new rules or being told that playing basketball was suddenly wrong."

"You were always new and on edge."

"That's exactly it." He sighed, then seemed to realize everything that he'd just said. "Wow. I'm so sorry, Betsy. Here we were having such a good time and I just dumped all that in your lap. I don't know why I did that."

"I'd like to think you did because you knew I could handle it." Leaning closer, she added, "I'm really glad you shared your feelings with me too."

He rolled his eyes. "Yeah, right."

"I mean it. August, for most of my life I was coddled and protected. I've been told that I was delicate. I felt like my brother and my parents took great pains to make sure I never did anything that might strain my lungs . . . but they transferred those worries to the rest of my body. I was guarded and protected in every sense of the word. I like that you're treating me as someone who can help you." Fearing that she might have said too much, she added, "I mean, that you can depend on."

Reaching out, he clasped her hands. "I don't know what's going on between us, Betsy . . . everything seems to be happening so fast." He swallowed. "But I sure don't want to second-guess it. I need to tell you something."

Her heart started beating fast. "Okay."

"Betsy, I really like you."

"I . . . I like you too." She was sure her face was beet red, but she didn't care. The things that they were sharing meant so much. Honestly, their conversations felt more intimate than if they'd been spending their time locked in an embrace.

"So, are you ready to take a walk, look at pelicans, and then get some lunch?"

"I am — if you can take the time to do that. I know you have to work."

"I'm going to make the time. It's important to me."

When their eyes met again, Betsy felt like they were agreeing to so much more than just a walk and a bite to eat. It felt like they were agreeing to something new and precarious and special.

They were agreeing to a future.

17

The morning was as beautiful as the forecasters had predicted. It was sunny, not too humid, and still in the low seventies at ten in the morning. Stretching out on her towel on what had become her favorite part of the beach on Siesta Key, Annie sipped her coffee. Every time she made the effort to get up early, gather her things together, and then ride the SCAT to this particular beach, she was glad she did.

Annie enjoyed watching everyone take morning walks, set up a play area for their children, or simply do what she was doing — sipping coffee and counting her blessings.

She had so many to count too. Now that she was in the middle of her second week of vacation, Annie could honestly say that coming to stay for a month with Danielle had been one of the best decisions she'd ever made. The two of them were having a great time getting to know each other again.

Okay, saying it was "great" might be a bit of an exaggeration — but they'd made huge progress in mending their fractured relationship. In addition to finding a restaurant they both enjoyed called The Boardwalk, they'd also begun to cook dinners together.

Learning how much they enjoyed cooking in the kitchen together had come as a surprise to both of them. Annie had never realized how good of a cook Danielle was.

Danielle, in turn, had said that she hadn't realized what a great baker Annie was. So far Annie had made three loaves of bread. On those nights, Danielle grilled fish and made a large salad, and they'd spend the evening on the patio eating the freshly grilled fish, munching on salad, and dipping the fresh bread, still warm from the oven, in olive oil.

Sometimes they sipped wine. Most of the time they drank seltzer water or lemonade or tea. They laughed and giggled every single time, though.

She was really going to miss those meals.

Of course, another reason why they'd been able to mend their long rift was Betsy. Helping Betsy learn to swim had united them toward a goal. In addition, focusing on the sweet girl had given them something amazing to concentrate on besides themselves. Or the mistakes each of them had made in their relationship. Annie knew God had been working with them too. His grace had helped each of them learn to let go of past guilt and regrets.

Betsy's lessons hadn't been all fun and games, though. Progress was slow and she was often scared and tentative.

Danielle was infinitely patient with her but firm too. They'd soon realized that they had to tag team in order to get her to make progress. Though usually Danielle was in charge, sometimes Annie would lead Betsy's lessons for a few minutes and Danielle would watch. The variety seemed to keep all three of them from getting frustrated.

So, every moment of Betsy's lessons wasn't easy, but the results were so worth it. Betsy could put her head under the water and swim a few basic strokes. It was a huge accomplishment.

Annie glanced at her watch and breathed a sigh of relief. She still had almost two more hours until she had to leave. Betsy was coming over at one o'clock. Annie had told Danielle she'd be back by noon to help her set up and do a quick clean of the bathroom, kitchen, and patio.

Remembering the two cinnamon sugar

donuts she'd bought at the bakery near the SCAT stop, Annie sipped her coffee. Did she want one of them now . . . or did she want to wait another fifteen minutes?

"Hey. You're back."

Glancing up at the man who'd just spoken, Annie practically choked on her coffee. "I am," she blurted. "It's Jack, right?"

He grinned. "Yep. And you're Annie."

He was still as handsome as he was the first time they'd talked. She smiled up at him. "How goes the family reunion in the pink motel?"

"Truth?"

"Of course."

"Exhausting." The lines around Jack's eyes deepened as he laughed. "I don't know if you have kids, but I don't. So, while I love all my nieces and nephews, they wear me out."

"I don't have kids either, so I can relate. I bet you're sleeping well at night."

"I am. Like a log."

She playfully glanced at the horizon. "Where are they all now? I would've thought you wouldn't be able to leave the motel without a child or two by your side."

"That was the case, but most of them left yesterday. The only kids still here are teenagers, and they have better things to do than hang around with their uncle." He smiled. "I'm on my own for another two weeks."

"That's so nice." Realizing how she sounded, Annie said, "I mean, I know you'll miss your family, but I'm glad that you're going to get a chance to relax too."

"Don't worry, I know what you meant . . . and I feel the same way. I'm moving to a rental house today and will work from there. Honestly, I don't think I want to go home. Toledo is pretty this time of year, but Lake Erie's beaches can't compare to this place."

"I'm feeling the same way."

Jack gestured to the sand. "Do you mind if I sit here with you for a moment? Or is that too much?"

"I don't mind." She smiled up at him. "If I'm being honest, I was afraid you were going to ask me to go for a walk on the beach."

"That's not your thing?"

"It is, but at the moment I don't want to do much beyond sit and sip my coffee."

He sat down next to her and stretched out his legs as well, giving her the opportunity to notice that he was not only tan but was wearing a pair of dark plum swim trunks, a gray T-shirt, and a pair of black flip-flops.

"So, what do you do, Annie?"

She put down the cup she'd been holding. "I'm currently a blogger and make videos on YouTube and TikTok."

His eyebrows rose. "Really? What do you video? Dance moves or something?"

She laughed. "If you're asking me that, I'm guessing that you're not very active on those platforms."

"I'm not." He winced. "Like, not at all."

"Well, to answer your question, I make videos and blogs about easy ways to save money."

"And?" He raised his eyebrows.

"And, believe it or not, they're popular enough that I have followers and sponsors. It's fun."

Jack still looked confused. "I didn't realize that a person could make a living doing that." He grinned suddenly. "I guess I should start watching your videos, huh?"

"That's what I usually say to skeptics."

"How did you get into this?"

"The short version is that I used to teach high school and then I worked in a law office. I got tired of the stress, of commuting, and spending my days making other people happy. So I decided to quit. But then I had to figure out how to make a life for myself on my terms."

"Which is how you started saving money."

"Yep. I got creative, and it worked. The more I saved, the more I tried to find more ways to do that. So, I started to follow various people's Instagram accounts and blogs, but no one was doing things like I was doing. That's when I started my own blog. It kind of blew up from there." Feeling like she'd just given him a commercial, she said, "What about you? What do you do?"

"Nothing near as interesting as you. I'm an analyst for a Fortune 500 company."

"What do you analyze?" As soon as she asked, Annie wondered if she should've already known. Had she just sounded stupid?

Not looking perturbed in the slightest, Jack leaned back on his hands. "Among other things, I study trends, examine data, and scrutinize performance output. Every so often I make suggestions to the board and other investors."

He sounded successful and smart. "Wow. That's really impressive." She chuckled. "Would it be rude to admit that I didn't expect you to have a job like that?"

Jack pretended to look offended. "Really? What made you think that? Was it the scruffy hair and beard? Or the fact that I've been half covered in sand and saltwater every time we've talked?"

"It might be a toss-up." She smiled so he would know that she was teasing.

"I don't know about you, but I kind of enjoy exceeding expectations."

"I feel the same way." She reached for her cup and sipped — but discovered it was empty. "So what are you going to do the rest of your vacation?"

"Hopefully take a certain pretty blogger out to lunch or dinner at least once."

He was asking her out? "Oh."

"Sorry. Are you seeing someone?" He frowned slightly. "Or, ah, if you're not interested, I get it. We just met on the beach. Joining me for a meal might be weird."

Was it? She wasn't sure what the "right" way to date was anymore. She paused, wondering if she should lie since he was already giving her a way out. But she didn't want to lie — or even be thought of as a woman who spoke with guys on the beach when she had a boyfriend at home.

What she was realizing was that she didn't want to say no.

Annie knew it was time to stop carrying around her broken heart from Clay. Past time. Thinking of Betsy's life list, she decided that dating again, even dating that might not lead to a serious relationship, should be on her list.

"I could do lunch," she said at last. "I'd like that."

"What about today? Like around two?"

"I can't this afternoon. My sister and I are giving swimming lessons."

"Really? Do you do that often?"

"Not at all. This opportunity kind of fell in our laps. It's going well, though."

"It sounds like there's a story there."

"There is. I'll tell you about it when we have lunch."

"Would it be okay for me to get your number so I can text you?"

"Sure."

He pulled out his phone and tapped in her number then texted her. "Now you'll know who this is when I text you later today." He stood up. When he looked down at her, his expression seemed warmer. "I'm glad I saw you again, Annie."

She watched him walk away down the beach. His flip-flops were in one hand as he walked on the edge of the surf. She half expected him to dive in — and maybe he would have if he didn't have his cell phone.

Leaning back on her elbows, she closed her eyes and simply let the sun's rays warm her skin. She was going to have to figure out a way to tell Danielle about Jack and her lunch date.

If it really happened. Danielle shouldn't be annoyed, but one never knew how she would react to anything. Mentally shrugging, she decided not to worry about it. She was fascinated by Jack and wanted to get to know him better. There was nothing wrong with that. Nothing wrong at all.

18

The day was sunny, warm, and not even too humid. It was a nice change of pace. Someone was mowing the grass next door. Kids were giggling nearby. Every so often, their squeals and laughter would ring out, meshing with the seagulls' squawking in the air.

Betsy hardly noticed any of that. Instead, practically all she could hear was Danielle. She was treading water right next to Betsy and speaking in a kind but firm tone. Her voice was also loud enough to drown out most of the other noises surrounding them. As well as the little voice in Betsy's head that was telling her that she should stop.

She really wanted to stop.

As her strokes slowed to a mere crawl, Danielle moved closer. "Come on, Betsy, you can do it. Just a little bit further."

Honestly, Danielle was beginning to sound a whole lot like a drill sergeant. It was becoming irritating.

Betsy didn't want to swim another stroke. She was exhausted, and they were heading toward the deep end. Even though her brain was telling her that there was no way she was about to sink like a rock, a good portion of the rest of her was pretty sure that it was a possibility.

Reaching out an arm, she found the side of the pool and gripped it tight. It took her a few seconds to catch her breath. Luckily, Danielle didn't say a word. She continued to tread water like she hadn't been doing that for the last half hour.

"How are you doing?" Danielle asked at last.

"I'm tired," she said honestly.

"Tired is to be expected, but what about the rest of you? Do you feel dizzy? Are you having trouble breathing?"

Taking stock, Betsy realized that she was breathing hard from physical exertion, not because of an upcoming asthma attack. "I feel a little winded, but it's nothing bad."

"Do you promise?"

Betsy almost smiled. During their second lesson, Danielle and Annie had both made her promise that she wouldn't try to hide her breathing issues from them. "Promise."

"Let's go, then. You still have half a pool length to go."

Which was her problem. Turning her head, she gazed at the deep end of the pool. It currently looked as treacherous as what she imagined the middle of the Pacific Ocean was like. "I don't know if I can, Danny. I don't think I'm strong enough."

"Nope, that's not allowed. You're not allowed to say you can't."

"But —"

Danielle shook her head again. "Betsy, you promised me when we first got in that you wouldn't psych yourself out. I'm going to hold you to it. Now, come on. Let go of the side and swim toward me."

"But it's really deep." She knew she sounded pitiful, but being scared was scared.

"That's why we're going to swim and not try to walk on water." She motioned Betsy forward with her hands. "I promise, you can do this. Come on now."

Betsy knew Danielle was right there and wouldn't let anything happen to her. Unfortunately, the rest of her body wasn't so sure. Actually, she was beginning to think that she had broken out in a cold sweat, which was remarkable, given that the temperature was in the midnineties. "B-but what if I . . ." Her voice drifted off.

Annie, who was sitting on the ledge just a

few feet away, spoke to her. "Betsy, not only is Danny right there, but I'm watching too. Neither of us are going to let anything happen to you. Just like you've promised to be honest about your health, I'm being honest about how seriously we take our responsibility to look out for you. But . . . you have to try. This is on your life list."

"I know."

"Then, come on! You don't want to quit, do you?"

"Nee. B-but you two don't understand how hard this is for me."

Danielle raised an eyebrow. "You're right. I learned to swim when I was really little, not an adult." Her voice turned haughty. "However, I do know how hard it is to decide to open one's house to a stranger and attempt to teach her how to swim while I'm on vacation. How about that?"

Shocked, Betsy sucked in a breath. "That's not fair. I'm paying you."

"Do you really want to talk about the going prices for swim lessons, dear? Because I have news for you — they are not ten dollars an hour." She clapped her hands twice. "Now come on, Betsy. Start swimming. Or if you really don't want to swim, get out of the pool."

"Y-you'd do that?"

"Yeah. You're wasting my time."

Betsy glared at both of them. Why were they being so mean? And especially Danielle? Up until now, Danny had been so sweet and encouraging. Irritated, she pushed off and started swimming the breaststroke toward the end of the pool. She didn't look at Danielle and ignored whatever Annie was calling out.

As her anger kicked in, she even increased her speed, mainly just to show the women that she was working hard and it wasn't going to be her fault if she drowned while she was in the pool.

When she got to the far end at last, she held on to the ledge in a death grip, panting.

Only then did she notice that the other two women were clapping and cheering.

Looking at them both in surprise, she glared. "You did that on purpose, D-Danielle! Y-you said all those mean things so I'd stop whining."

Holding on to the side with one hand, Danielle grinned. "Yep. I did."

"I-I can't believe you."

"Sorry, but you needed to feel something other than scared."

"And maybe a little self-pity," Annie added.

She hated to admit that she'd been letting both of those things fill her, but she couldn't deny the truth. "I . . . I guess it worked."

"It sure did." Danielle gracefully pulled herself up out of the pool. "You swam like a pro. I'm really proud of you."

It took a moment for her to realize that she was proud of herself too. "Thank you for being so tough."

Annie laughed. "Slide over to the ladder and come on out. Your lesson is over, tiger."

"Already?"

"Yep. Hey, would you like to stay for a snack? I bought some cheese and crackers."

"Thank you, but I'm going to have lunch with my girlfriend Mary. I've been so busy with my golf and swimming lessons, we haven't spent much time together."

"Is Mary learning to play golf too?"

"Oh no. She has no interest in golf. Besides, she's pregnant. I don't think she wants to do much besides sleep and dream about her baby."

"That sounds familiar," Danielle said with a soft expression.

"I didn't know you had children, Danielle."

"I do. Their names are Phil and Travis." Her voice softened. "Phil is short for Ophelia. My daughter never cared for that name, though."

Danielle sounded so sad.

"Do they live near your home?"

"Oh no. They're all grown up." She smiled again, but it didn't reach her eyes. "I wish things were different, but I don't see them much anymore."

Betsy dried off, took a sip of water, then put on her dress over her damp bathing suit. Once again, Annie and Danielle watched as she pinned the front together. They seemed fascinated with the notion of not having buttons.

"I like that bright turquoise color on you," Danielle said. "I think it makes your dark hair and eyes pop."

"Thank you. This dress is one of my favorites."

After she paid her ten dollars and hugged them both goodbye, she walked out the front door. Sometimes she accepted a ride from one of the sisters, but today she was feeling like a walk was in order.

The more she thought about how she'd complained, the worse she felt. Betsy had always prided herself on being tougher than most people imagined and not whining even when she was at her sickest. But she'd been almost ready to give up today. Worse, she was trying to put the blame on Annie and

Danielle instead of on her own weaknesses. She didn't care for that one bit.

She thought about it some more while she walked to the SCAT stop, waited for the bus to arrive, then rode it from Longboat Key to the stop right outside Yoder's.

Once again, she was surrounded by Amish men and women. Some were shopping at Yoder's fruit and vegetable stand, others were in line at the restaurant. Most of the folks, though, were either simply walking, bicycling on the sidewalk, or chatting with their friends.

When she noticed two Amish girls about her age chatting on cell phones, she decided to do the same thing. The casual atmosphere in Pinecraft really did let all kinds of "normal" Amish rules go by the wayside. She wanted to talk to her mother but didn't want to do it within hearing distance of Mary.

Her mother answered immediately. "Betsy, are you all right?"

That was always the way her mother greeted her. It would have been humorous if her mother didn't sound so frantic. "I'm fine. I just finished my swimming lesson. I'm sitting on a park bench near Yoder's."

"You're on your cell phone?"

"Jah. A couple of folks are giving me dark

191

looks, but most aren't paying me no mind. Other Amish men and women are doing the same thing."

"Why are you calling from there? Is Mary not liking you using her phone so much?"

"She doesn't mind. I wanted to talk to you about something, though." She took a deep breath. "Mamm, I almost gave up today."

"Hold on. I'm trying to keep up. You almost gave up what?"

"Learning to swim. I was in the water and Danielle was encouraging me to swim the whole length of the pool. When I was near the deep end, I got scared. Mamm, I didn't want to go."

"She shouldn't have asked you to do that. You could've drowned!"

Some of the hope Betsy had been feeling faded away. She'd wanted her mother to be encouraging and proud of her — not act as if Betsy wasn't capable of swimming a couple of feet. "Nee, Mamm. I wasn't going to drown. All I had to do was swim the same stroke that I did in the shallower part of the pool. I know how to swim the breaststroke real well. The problem was that I didn't believe in myself."

"Well, don't keep me in suspense. What happened?"

Betsy smiled. "Danielle made me mad on purpose. She told me that she was giving up her valuable time teaching a stranger in her house how to swim. And that she wasn't getting paid much for it, either."

"Oh my." Humor entered her voice. "And that didn't set well with you, I gather?"

"Not at all." She took a deep breath. "Mamm, I acted as spoiled as a toddler wanting another piece of cake. I couldn't believe that they weren't coddling me."

Her mother started laughing. "So . . ."

"So, I showed them and swam the whole way."

"Good for you."

"They clapped and cheered like I just won a swim meet or something. I'm so embarrassed." Of course, she was also feeling proud of herself too.

"I don't think you have anything to be embarrassed about. A lot of adults are afraid of being in deep water — even deep pool water."

"I know. But Mamm, I'm more embarrassed about my reaction. I acted like such a child. It made me realize that I leaned on you and Daed to protect me too much. I'm going to continue to push myself to do more new things."

"Such as what?"

There was an edge to her mother's voice now. Betsy didn't blame her for sounding defensive. She had just told her mother that she and her daed were partly to blame for her hang-ups. But that didn't mean she was going to hide her feelings or her goals. Not any longer. "I'm going to continue working on my life list. I want to do things."

"Don't forget about your limits, Betsy."

"Mamm, what I'm trying to tell you is that I don't think my physical limits have been stopping me. My emotional ones have been the problem. I want to be a woman to be proud of."

"You already are. You know, I don't know who made you feel like you weren't special." Sounding testy, she asked, "Was it your new girlfriends? Have they made you feel like you need to be different? If so, I think that you ought to step back. Daed and I will even be happy to send you some money so you don't have to stay —"

Betsy cut her off. "Don't say it, Mamm. Not a bit of what I'm going through is Mary Margaret's or Lilly's or even Esther's fault."

"So, you're saying it's mine? Mine and your father's?"

Boy, she wished she hadn't decided to open up to her mother. "Nee, Mamm. The fault lies with me. Not you." Feeling de-

194

feated, she leaned back against the bench's back. "I better go."

"I think we should talk about this more. And maybe we should think about cutting your trip short?"

"I'll call in a couple of days."

"Betsy, don't be like this. Remember Philippians 4:19."

She knew that verse by heart. "God will use His wonderful riches in Christ Jesus to give you everything you need." She loved that verse and believed in it too. But she absolutely did not want it to be tossed out at the end of a difficult conversation. "Do not start quoting Bible verses, Mamm."

"Betsy, you're getting all worked up. Do you have your inhaler?"

She rolled her eyes. "I love you. Goodbye." When she realized her mother was inhaling, obviously about to deliver another speech, she disconnected.

Stuffing the phone in her pocket, Betsy realized that she was breathing hard and her lungs were feeling tight. She needed to relax. Even though her heart was beating fast and she was ready to pace back and forth on the sidewalk, she made herself lean back again and take a couple of deep, cleansing breaths. After her third one, she could feel her body start to ease.

Finally she became aware of her surroundings again. The day was still sunny, and most everyone was going about their business. She was pretty sure she recognized Nate, August's friend, talking to a blond server who worked at Yoder's. They seemed completely entranced with each other. In addition, there were some small Amish girls playing with a bottle of bubbles and an older man walking his dog. A pair of Englischer tourists were trying to take pictures without blatantly taking pictures of anyone who was Amish. All were familiar sights. The world hadn't changed — only her perspective of it had.

That was the only difference.

However, she was starting to realize that was all it took to see the world — and herself — in a whole new way.

19

It was a near perfect day in Pinecraft. There was hardly a cloud in the sky, the humidity was low, and because it was summer, the tourist crowds were light. Nate hardly noticed. As far as he was concerned, a hurricane could be approaching and he would still think it was a great day.

Honestly, any day spent in Brianna's company was a good one. For the first time in his life, he was obsessed with a girl. He was pretty certain that he wasn't going to be able to work or golf or spend any time with his friends until Brianna was his girlfriend. Nate couldn't stop thinking about her. Every time they talked, Brianna looked into his eyes in a dreamy way. He reckoned he was probably looking at her the same way.

It seemed no shame was involved when it came to falling in love.

Especially at this moment, since he'd left

work at the hardware store early just so he could see Brianna during her fifteen-minute afternoon break. She'd obviously been delighted to see him — she'd greeted him with a bright smile. That smile had hit him smack in the middle of his chest and gave him a much-needed burst of hope for their future. If things continued to go smoothly between them, anything was possible.

Except, perhaps, privacy.

Standing together on the street right outside of Yoder's, Nate knew they were being watched by just about every person who was either standing in line or walking by. He didn't care, but it was obvious that Brianna did.

Her eyes kept darting around as if she was worried about who was seeing them together.

Finally, he began to feel a little irritated. "Bri, are you worried about your friends seeing us together?"

She bit her bottom lip. "Oh no. Have I been that obvious?"

"Yes." He smiled to let her know that he wasn't mad — just confused. "Is there a reason you want to keep our relationship a secret?"

"It has nothing to do with me."

Which made no sense at all. "I think

you're going to have to clarify that."

She made an irritated noise. "Nate, it's my mother. She's so goofy!"

"What's she doing?"

"She's determined that you and I should court the way she and mei daed did. With a chaperone and only at our house."

"That's it?" He'd sit on her front porch with both her parents watching if that's what it took to court her. But it did seem a bit much.

"Maybe, eventually, we could go on supervised walks."

Supervised walks? "Brianna. We're too old for that, and no one does that anymore. Even my grandparents would say such restrictions aren't necessary."

She chuckled. "I think my grandparents would agree with yours." She lowered her voice, like she feared someone would overhear. "Mommi and Dawdi have always thought my mother was a bit of a prissy sort. They've even told her that to her face!"

"I'm guessing that didn't go over well?"

"Not at all." She waved a hand in the air. "What can we do, though? I live at home and I need to follow my parents' rules."

"What's going to happen if someone you know spies us standing here together?"

"And they tell mei mamm?" When he

nodded, she bit her lip again. "I'm not sure."

She looked so worried. "Brianna, I want to court you any way that I can, so I'll do my best to follow your mother's wishes, but I want to see you more often. Seeing you during your breaks at work isn't enough for me."

Her pretty blue eyes shone. "I want to see you more too."

He thought hard. "I'm going to talk to my parents. Maybe my mother can speak to yours about what a good guy I am."

"You are, but it probably won't help too much."

When she looked ready to bite down on her lip again, Nate acted without thinking. "Don't," he murmured, pressing his thumb on the spot where her teeth usually dug in. "You're going to make your lip bleed." And then he made matters worse by allowing his thumb to linger on that lip for another second.

Just as a woman approached.

"Oh no," Brianna murmured. "She's our neighbor. Prepare yourself."

"Hello, Brianna!"

"Hello, Marla," she squeaked. "It's a nice day, ain't so?"

That seemed to be all the opening Marla needed, and she walked right over and

200

introduced herself. "Young man, I've seen you around Pinecraft, but I don't think we've ever met."

"No, I don't think we have. I'm Nate Beachy."

"I've heard about you. You're the young man who came calling the other day."

"Yes."

"And now here you both are. Together again."

Brianna was bright red. Nate started talking fast. "Just for a moment. Brianna has a break and I just got off work." He sent the woman a meaningful, not exactly subtle look.

Luckily, she caught it. "Well, now, I'd best get going."

When she walked on, Brianna pressed her hand to her chest and started laughing. "Oh my word. I just about had a heart attack!"

"I hope not. I want you around," he teased. "Seriously, let me speak to my parents, okay? Maybe they can convince yours to let you come over every once in a while."

"What would we do then?"

"Sit on my front porch — but without a chaperone."

"All right. Now, I really should be going."

"I should too. See you soon."

She smiled at him again before darting inside. He stood there like the besotted fool he was, then turned to see Betsy walking by herself. She looked upset. Knowing how much August cared about her, Nate knew he couldn't pretend he didn't notice her.

"Betsy?"

She turned. "Yes? Oh, Nate. Hello again."

He smiled at her. "I wasn't sure you'd recognize me away from the course."

"I noticed you when you were speaking to that server outside Yoder's."

"You noticed us too?"

"Too? Who else were you aware of?" She brightened. "Is August nearby?"

"Hmm? Oh nee. I meant that one of Brianna's neighbors saw us talking and stopped by to say hello."

"Oh."

Feeling like he was talking gibberish, he tried to explain. "Brianna's parents like her to be chaperoned when she's around callers. Or whenever she speaks to me, I guess."

Betsy's eyes danced. "But you aren't fifteen."

Her comment was the last thing he would've expected. "What in the world does that mean?"

"Oh, um . . . d-did I embarrass you?" She started walking.

"Not at all. I'm just not sure what you meant. Really," he added so she wouldn't think he was being a jerk or something. Since he didn't have anything else to do and wanted to get her perspective, Nate decided to walk by her side.

After scanning his face again — obviously to make sure he was being honest — she shrugged. "Well, in my church district, chaperones watch all the teenagers like hawks . . . but by the time they turn eighteen or nineteen, things loosen up a lot."

"I don't remember my parents ever being so cautious, not even with my older brother, and he was a bit of a handful at fifteen." He shrugged. "Anyway, Brianna was just going back to work when I noticed that you didn't look too happy. I wanted to make sure you were all right."

"Danke. I'm fine." She exhaled. "Sort of. I . . . I was talking with my mother on the phone, and she's decided that I should come home early. We got into a bit of an argument."

"But what about your golf lessons?"

She giggled. "I know! I haven't even played a full round of golf yet. Not that it would go very well. I can hardly tee off."

"All the more reason to stay, ain't so?" he asked as they stopped at a crosswalk. Cars were driving through the intersection, along with a good amount of Amish pedaling bikes — and a couple were even riding the new, gasoline-powered bicycles that were all the rage.

She chuckled while the crosswalk "wait" signal continued to beep. "There's more reasons than that. I've been learning to swim and ride a bike. I've been doing a lot of things on my life list." Looking sheepish, she added, "Plus, there's August."

He was enough of a gentleman not to make her spell out what she meant. He was also enough of a friend to not divulge just how much August liked her. August would be really bummed if she went home early. "You've got to stay."

"Danke for saying that. Being here is important to me. I fit in and I'm happy. But my parents have done so much for me, I don't want to upset them."

"You're only going to be here for a month, right?"

She nodded.

"Then you need to finish what you started," he added as they started walking again. "Sorry to disagree with your parents, but you're obviously happy and following through on your plans. If they don't want you doing that, then maybe the problem is with them instead of you?"

"That's a good point." She stopped in front of a pale blue house with a profusion of begonias and impatiens planted in the front garden. "Well, this is my friend Mary's house. I'd better go in. Thank you for walking me back."

"I'm glad we saw each other. Believe it or not, talking with you made some things clearer in my head."

She grinned. "Glad to be of service."

He waited until Betsy got inside, then decided to walk over to the golf course. He needed more time to walk and figure out what he was going to say to his parents. They would be helpful but they were also going to want all the information.

Which meant he was finally going to have to let his family in on his secret — that he'd had the biggest crush on Brianna Lapp for months, finally made his move, and now needed their help.

He really hoped they would decide to do just that — instead of tease him about his awkward courting.

20

Aunt Diane had made August's favorite supper. It was simple but fresh and excellent — noodles with butter and cheese, green beans, and a piece of perfectly seasoned grilled grouper. Diane really had a way with fish.

All three of them had found the time to sit down together too. That was a minor miracle, since usually one of them stayed at the pro shop to greet golfers coming off the course or to supervise the driving range.

However, about four months ago he and Uncle Gideon had talked about both their time and how well the golf course was doing financially. They'd agreed that it was time to start enjoying their evenings more — and also time to focus on their personal lives instead of just the golf course.

With that in mind, August had recently hired two teenagers to help out. Within two weeks, the boys had gotten the hang of things and become really good workers. Both August and his uncle had wondered why they hadn't done that years ago.

The boys were doing a good job and liked hanging out at the golf course at night. Their customers seemed to enjoy the boys' enthusiasm too. They were generally happy, were good conversationalists, and were respectful to the golfers.

Uncle Gideon had even begun giving them some golf lessons and tips from time to time. It was obvious that they'd be pretty decent golfers one day. As a bonus, they were also encouraging their many friends and family members to come to the course more often. It was something of a win-win for everyone.

Since the boys were happily in charge of the driving range that evening and he was eating his favorite supper, August knew that he should be happy. And he would be . . . if his mother hadn't just Skyped to deliver some terrible news.

His father had been injured while riding with a local into the village. August still wasn't sure of the specifics, but it had something to do with a motorbike, some stray dogs, and a car with faulty brakes. He had been taken to the hospital for surgery.

To make matters worse, his mother hadn't

been willing to speak to either Diane or Gideon, so August had to relay the news when he got off the computer. Diane had listened to the news with a stricken expression before quietly turning away.

But not before he'd spied tears in her eyes.

Now they were eating supper in near silence. Aunt Diane was upset, Uncle Gideon was fuming, and August felt even more emotions — worry, guilt, irritation, and sadness.

"Did your mother mention when she was going to Skype again?" Gideon asked.

August shook his head. "Nee. We usually set a date and time for the next Skype, but of course she was too upset to do that. I'll have to keep checking on your computer to see if she sets up another call."

Though he still looked angry, his uncle seemed to pull himself together. "I know she won't want the expense, but I reckon Charity will use the phone if things get worse with David," Gideon said.

"Jah. I suppose she will." However, the three of them knew that an actual phone call was a long shot. Not only would the connection be difficult but the price would be astronomical.

"We should pray for David," Diane said. She held out her hands to both August and

Gideon. They clasped hers as they bowed their heads.

August prayed for his father's recovery and the hospital workers' healing hands. He also prayed for the other people involved in the accident and his mother. Finally, he prayed for Diane. He truly hoped she would eventually find some way to accept her brother's unfair anger toward her. He'd long ago given up asking the Lord to change his parents' hearts. They were determined to never forgive Gideon and Diane for taking him in and encouraging him to have a successful career at the golf course. As far as his parents were concerned, Gideon and Diane had played a large role in August's fall from grace.

When each of them had lifted their heads, August was relieved to see that his aunt looked a little less burdened. He took another bite of noodles. "This supper is so gut, Diane. Danke for making all my favorites."

Aunt Diane gave him a watery smile. "It was no trouble. Gideon and I like this meal as well."

Gideon cleared his throat. "When will you see your student again?"

"Do you mean Betsy?"

"Of course I mean Betsy," Uncle Gideon

replied with a laugh. "Do you have plans to see her again?"

"I do. I'll see her in a couple of days."

"Just for a lesson?"

"Jah. A lesson then lunch."

"You two should do something else together," Diane said. "Take her to the beach or to the botanical gardens. Something fun."

"Or go calling at her house," Gideon murmured. "Now that the boys are here, you have time to visit Betsy in the evening."

Calling? Like a formal suitor? "She's staying at a friend's house. Wouldn't that be strange?"

"Nee," Diane said. "Besides, I think it would be the right and proper thing to do. Didn't you mention that she's staying with a friend who is married?"

"Jah."

"Then her friend and her friend's husband would probably like to meet ya."

Realizing how he'd made formal calls sound as fun as catching the flu, August shifted in his seat. It looked like he would soon be eating his words.

"What do you think about that idea?" Diane pressed. "I mean, you like her a lot, jah?"

He didn't exactly want to discuss his feelings for Betsy, but his aunt and uncle would probably be the best people to talk things over with. They had such an open, refreshing outlook on life. "I want to see Betsy more often, but I'm not sure about a formal call."

"Why not?"

"I don't know what our future could be like."

"What do you mean?" Diane waved a hand. "Obviously, I know that she lives in Kentucky and you live here, but there's no reason one of you can't move if you two get serious enough to think about marriage."

When he noticed Gideon nodding as well, August looked at him in surprise. "You'd be okay with me moving?"

"Do I want you to move? Nee. But would I understand if you had to move? Jah."

"I'm not even sure what I would do in Hart County, Kentucky."

"I reckon they play golf there too, August."

"Yes, but . . ." He stopped, feeling flummoxed. "I'll have to think about that."

"Indeed," Uncle Gideon murmured.

The phone ringing made all three of them freeze. "I'll get it," August said.

There was every possibility someone was calling about the golf course — or it could even be another relative or friend.

However, the feeling of dread in the pit of

his stomach told him it was likely something else.

Picking up the phone, he prayed he wasn't right.

But of course he was.

"August! Your father's condition is worse than we'd thought," Mamm blurted the moment he said hello.

He leaned against the wall for support. "What happened?"

"They just got back the results of his latest bloodwork. They think he contracted a terrible infection in the hospital. The doctors are trying to combat it, but they said he isn't out of the woods yet."

"Oh, Mamm."

She lowered her voice. "If your father doesn't get better, he could lose his leg."

August closed his eyes. "I'm sorry, Mamm. Gideon, Diane, and I were just praying for him. We'll continue to do so."

"We're going to need more than your prayers, son. I need you to come here."

He froze. "Why? Do you think Daed is going to get worse?" He simply couldn't ask if his mother thought his father was about to die.

"August, Daed and I want you to come here and help lead the mission."

"In Namibia?"

"Of course here." Turning all businesslike, she continued. "Now, if you call the headquarters, they'll help you find flights. It will be expensive, of course, but maybe you can use your savings to help with the costs. Or maybe your aunt and uncle can pay for the trip. I'm sure they have plenty of funds for that."

"Mamm, I can't go to Africa." Going to work in the mission wouldn't be a temporary thing. It would be a commitment of at least a year. A year doing what he never wanted to do again.

"Did you not hear what I said?" Her voice rose. "We need you, August. This mission needs you too."

It was almost physically painful to refuse, but he had no choice. But just as he opened his mouth to tell her no, he amended his words. "I . . . I need some time to think about this." Maybe that really was what he needed to do. Shouldn't he want to do what they asked?

"August, there is no time."

"I'm sorry, Mamm, but I'm not willing to drop everything to run the mission. I will think about it, though. I'll Skype you in a few days."

"I don't know what I'm going to tell your father. Or the mission headquarters. Or the villagers. I already told everyone that you would be here soon."

Hearing how upset she was about going back on her word almost made his decision easier. He'd always hated how she put his needs last . . . and she was doing it again.

"I guess you'll just have to tell them the truth, Mamm," he said at last. "You'll have to tell them that I grew up and have my own job and life that I can't leave at a moment's notice."

She hung up. Once again, she'd made sure that she didn't tell him that she loved him.

Tears pricked his eyes as he realized that such things still hurt.

21

At first, Betsy was sure a nightmare had woken her up. She'd been dreaming she was underwater and unable to signal to either Danielle or Annie for help. She'd kept reaching out a hand for them, but they'd ignored her. Her lungs had felt like they were about to burst.

Her futile attempt to call out had woken her up with a start. It took less than a second for her to realize what was happening. She was having an asthma attack.

Reaching out to her bedside table, she felt for her inhaler. It was where she always left it. Unfortunately, her jerky, bleary-eyed movements pushed the device down onto the floorboards. She was going to have to get out of bed and crawl around to find it.

Tears filled her eyes as she struggled to fill her lungs with air. Each breath burned. Pushing away the pain, she attempted to be positive. The Lord was with her. She could do what had to be done.

One leg out, two legs. She braced a hand on the mattress but mistook the space — and fell.

She cried out as she landed on her right knee.

"Betsy?" Mary called out. "Are you all right?"

No, she was not. "N-n-n!" Her stutter was back. She would've been mortified to sound so pathetic . . . if she wasn't struggling so much.

The bedroom door flew open. "Betsy! Oh my word. Jayson! Jayson!" Mary's voice became progressively more frantic as she knelt down by Betsy's side. "Betsy, can you hear me?"

Betsy tried to motion for her inhaler.

By the grace of God, Mary seemed to understand what she needed and bent down to look for it.

"Should I call 911?" Jayson asked from the doorway.

"You better. She doesn't look good. Oh my word," she mumbled. "Oh, thank the Lord. I found her inhaler. All right, Betsy, here we go."

Betsy could barely move her head to face Mary.

Her friend held the inhaler up. "Come on,

now. Don't give up. Help me, Betsy."

Betsy was hardly able to nod as Mary put the inhaler up to her lips and pressed. She inhaled, but her lungs had been struggling too long. She could barely inhale enough to get a small amount into her lungs.

"They're on their way," Jayson said as he joined them. He knelt next to his wife. "Betsy, hold on, okay?" he said. "I promise, we're getting you help. The ambulance is coming."

She tried to nod, but her body was shutting down. The world was turning black as she fought to breathe.

"Betsy, again!"

She opened her lips with a searing cough, and Mary placed the inhaler to her mouth again. When she pressed the button on the top, another small amount of medicine flowed into her lungs. Betsy coughed.

Coughing was a step in the right direction. She knew that. However, it was obvious that it wasn't enough to make a huge difference. Every bit of her felt heavy. It felt like too much effort to even hold her head up.

She closed her eyes just as she heard the faint call of the sirens.

Even though it was only half past seven in

the morning, Nate strode into the pro shop. "I came here as soon as I could this morning," he said.

"You didn't have to come over so early." Nate worked at a hardware store and didn't usually report to work until nine.

"Of course I did. I would've come over after I heard your message last night, but I figured you were already asleep. So, how are you? Are you okay?"

"I'm sorry I left that message for you. I probably shouldn't have." He'd just had to tell someone about his news, though. He'd been so upset.

"You still didn't answer my question. Are you okay?"

"Nee." August realized his voice sounded harsh, but he couldn't seem to get over his mother's words.

"What happened? You said your father has gotten worse?"

"Jah." He walked around to the other side of the counter, glad for once that they didn't have their usual early morning crowd teeing off. "Nate, I don't know what to do."

Nate clasped his arm. "Tell me again what your mother said."

"Well, first my father broke his leg in several places as well as a couple of fingers. He had to have surgery on his leg."

218

"Okay. And . . . ?"

"Now infection has settled in. It's bad." His voice turned hoarse. "Mamm isn't 100 percent certain, given the problems with language and all, but she fears that Daed might lose his leg . . . or that the infection could spread into his bloodstream." Which, of course, meant that there was a possibility of his father dying.

Nate's eyes were filled with sympathy. "I'm sorry. I'm sure you're worried sick."

"Jah. I am. I'm scared that he's so bad off in Africa. I . . . I know they have good doctors and hospitals there, but . . ."

"But it's not like here in America."

"Exactly." He swallowed the lump in his throat. "Nate, my mother told me something else too. It's made me so confused, I don't know what to do."

"What did she say?"

August drew a deep breath, hardly able to verbalize the words. "Mamm asked me to come there and help run the mission."

"She wants you to go to Africa?"

"Jah."

"Right away?"

"Yes. My mother doesn't want to leave. Of course, there's too much for her to do alone. She needs help. She feels that I'm the best choice."

Nate frowned. "That doesn't even make sense. You aren't a missionary."

"I'm not. But it's my daed who's hurt and my mother who's having to hold down the fort, if you will. She feels the responsibility heavy on her shoulders. The people they're serving are depending on them."

"But isn't there someone else? Someone from the mission who can go and help out?"

He had to remember that Nate had no understanding of how things worked when one was a missionary. "It's not like there are missionaries to spare, Nate. Everyone is already serving someplace else." He exhaled. "I understand how she feels."

Nate looked incredulous. "August, are you actually thinking about dropping everything and going to Africa?"

"I don't know if I am or I'm not." That, of course, was why he felt so guilty. Shouldn't he want to do whatever his parents needed him to do? Shouldn't he want to go help serve?

"I know you love your parents, August, but they haven't been supportive of you. Like, not even a little bit. I can't believe you're considering dropping everything here and moving to Africa."

August pursed his lips. He didn't disagree with his buddy, but it still didn't make things easier. "They're my parents, Nate."

Nate waved a hand. "What about the golf course?"

"I don't want to leave it, but my aunt and uncle can run it. They used to run it just fine without me."

"What do they have to say?"

"My aunt is worried about her brother and doesn't want me to leave — but they also understand about duty." He lowered his voice. "After all, they did their duty by taking me in."

"That was not the same thing at all, August. You've been a blessing to them. Not a burden. Why, Gideon gets to sleep in now. Even he's told me how much he appreciates that."

As much as he valued Nate being on his side, his friend's words weren't helping much. In fact, all they did was make him more confused. "Thanks for listening to me. I'll let you know what I decide to do."

Nate winced. "I'm sorry. I've been bossing you around instead of listening and being sympathetic."

Since that was an understatement, August grinned. "I'm glad you spoke your mind. I need your honesty."

Still looking guilty, Nate picked up a sleeve of golf balls from the counter. "Hey, why don't I hang out here with you for a while? I can help you put away stock."

"There's no need for you to do that."

"Or when you're ready to take a break, we'll go play a couple of holes. It might be good not to talk about anything besides getting a little white ball into a hole."

August was pretty sure that his buddy had a point. Playing golf relaxed him, and it was their usual go-to. But he wasn't up for it today. Besides, he had someone else on his mind. "Thanks. I wish I could, but I'm waiting for Betsy. She should be here any minute." He glanced at the clock. "Actually, she's fifteen minutes late."

"That's not like her, is it?"

"Nee. Not at all." Concerned that she'd decided not to show up, August wondered if he'd somehow offended her last time they were together. Just as he was about to replay everything they'd talked about in his head, he shook off that thought.

Stress about his parents was making him overthink things. Betsy must have simply lost track of time and was running late.

"Betsy's not going to stand me up. Besides, she's determined to play at least one full round of golf. I bet she'll be here pretty soon."

"I'll still hang around, just in case," Nate said.

In case of what? he thought sarcastically just as an Amish man about their age walked through the door.

"Hiya. You interested in playing golf today?"

"Nee. I'm looking for August Troyer."

"That's me. How may I help ya?"

It was obvious that the man was looking him over. Seeming to come to a conclusion, he stepped forward. "May I speak to you in private? It concerns Betsy Detweiler."

"This is my best friend Nate. You can tell me anything in front of him."

"Okay. First, ah, my name is Jayson Raber. I'm married to Mary Margaret, who's a good friend of Betsy's."

August was starting to grow more concerned. "Betsy's spoken of both of you several times."

Jayson shifted uncomfortably. "There's no good way to tell you this. Betsy had an asthma attack last night. She was struggling so badly, she knocked her inhaler off the bedside table, then she fell trying to get it. We had to call for an ambulance."

"Where is she now? Is she okay?"

"Jah. Jah, she's gonna be all right, I think. They admitted her. She'll be in the hospital at least until tomorrow afternoon."

He felt like he'd just fallen from a cliff. "That long?"

"She has a history of lung ailments. Everyone takes her attacks seriously."

"I see."

Nate spoke up. "Can August visit her? Is she allowed visitors?"

"I reckon so, though I should warn you that her parents are arriving any minute. They got permission to fly here."

"What does that mean? Do you think she's not going to want to see me or something?"

"I'm sorry, but it means that they're going to watch over you like a hawk. Betsy's said that they go a little overboard when it comes to her health."

"What do you think Betsy is going to want me to do?" August wanted to see her, but he didn't want to make things worse.

"I know she would like to see you, though she might be embarrassed that you've found out just how bad her lungs are."

"I'll be there soon, then."

A new appreciation shone in Jayson's eyes. "I was hoping that's what you'd say." He stuffed his hands in his pockets. "Neither mei frau nor Betsy will appreciate me saying this, but Betsy thinks a lot of you. If you

224

turn your back on her now? It would break her heart."

"I'm not going to do that."

"All right then. She's in room 228."

"I need to check in with my aunt and uncle to make sure the course is covered. I'll be there within a couple of hours."

"I'll see you there." After shaking both his and Nate's hands, Jayson turned toward the door.

August couldn't let him leave just yet. "Hey, Jayson?"

He turned. "Jah?"

"Thank you for coming over to tell me about Betsy."

He shrugged. "I knew if you cared about her, you'd want to know."

Watching him turn and walk out the door, August realized he felt a kinship with the guy even though they'd just met. He respected that Jayson would go to so much trouble for his wife's friend. He realized then and there that he would do the very same thing.

"Wow," Nate said when they were alone again. "Well, now you know why she's not here. I guess it puts everything with your parents into perspective, doesn't it?"

Unfortunately, August wasn't sure if it did. He loved his parents and he wanted to do right by them. But he realized that his feelings for Betsy were quickly becoming much more than admiration. He was well on his way to falling in love with her.

And that meant he didn't want to leave her side.

22

If she weren't so sick, Betsy would've tried to kick her parents out of the hospital. So far, they had argued with the nurses, offended the doctor, and even been rude to Jayson and Mary. Then, after alienating pretty much everyone, they'd proceeded to treat her like a young girl without a decent brain in her head.

Betsy knew her flaws well. Sometimes she stuttered. Sometimes she spoke her mind a little too forcefully. And she would agree with anyone that her lungs weren't in great shape compared to a lot of other people's.

However, she was very sure she possessed a good brain. The Lord had been generous with her that way.

Now, she sat in the hospital bed while her mother hovered over her. It was aggravating and so very exhausting too. Only the dark shadows under her mother's eyes kept Betsy from asking her to leave.

"Where is Daed?"

"Your father is conferring with the doctor."

"Why? Dr. Klimek was in here during his rounds this morning. I already spoke with him about everything. And Mamm, I already told you what he said."

"I know, but we had some questions."

"What questions? You didn't ask me anything!"

"Calm down, dear. We wanted to be sure we heard all the right information, so Daed walked down to his office to discuss your treatment program. And to make sure he spoke with your doctor at home."

"There was no need for Daed to do that."

"Of course there was." Her mother peered at Betsy over her glasses. "If you would have let us be in the room when he examined you, your father wouldn't have had to pay Dr. Klimek a special call." She sighed. "Not that he told us all that much."

"I'm a grown woman. Of course I didn't want you in the room."

Her mother waved a hand, as if Betsy were throwing a temper tantrum. "Elizabeth, you know that we all need to be on the same page. This isn't something new. Besides, we need to understand the full extent of your needs."

"My needs? Mamm, I had an asthma attack."

"It was more than that. Besides, we don't want you to leave here without making sure you're healthy enough to travel."

Travel? "But I'm not going to travel anytime soon. I have almost two more weeks here."

"Betsy, don't be foolish. Of course you can't stay with your friends any longer."

"Why not? I'm fine now. The doctor said that my episode was just one of those things. I probably would've been fine if I hadn't been dreaming and then knocked over my inhaler."

"He said probably. Not definitely. There's a difference."

"Don't speak to me like I'm a child."

Her mother's expression hardened. "Don't you realize how selfish you're being? Mary Margaret is pregnant. You being here is putting undue stress on her. And her poor husband had to take off work today just to look after her and you."

"He's in construction. And since I'm currently here in the hospital, there's not anything either of them need to do for me."

"That's beside the point. Betsy, the truth is that you have overstayed your welcome. I know it and you know it. Mary Margaret is no doubt too kind to tell you any different."

Betsy blinked to stop the sudden burst of wetness that threatened to form in her eyes. Was she being selfish?

When her door opened, she sighed in relief. At this point, she would welcome a nurse coming in to draw more blood. Anything would be better than to be forced to continue the conversation.

She could hardly believe it when she saw that it wasn't another nurse. It was someone far better.

"Betsy. Praise God!" August exclaimed. "I've been wandering around the hallway for five minutes. I was starting to think I was never going to find your room number."

She gaped at him. "I can't believe you're here."

He strode right to her bedside and reached for her hand. "Jayson came to the pro shop this morning. He told Nate and me all about what happened. I couldn't believe it. How are you?"

He hadn't noticed her mother. He hadn't even seen her. He only had eyes on her. All the tension that had been building inside her dissipated.

Looking into his beautiful gray eyes, she smiled up at him. "I'm better now. I'm so glad to see you. Thank you for coming."

"There's nowhere else I'd rather be. Now, tell me all about what happened, that is, if you can talk all right."

She smiled. "I can talk just fine."

"Now, do you need anything before I get settled? Do you need some water first?"

"You can introduce yourself to me, young man."

August's eyes were so wide it was funny. Dropping her hand, he turned and faced her mother, who was glaring at him. "Ah . . . hello. I'm sorry. I didn't see you in here."

"That is very obvious."

"August, please meet my mother, Fawn Detweiler. Mamm, this is August Troyer. He's my golf teacher." She winked at him.

August chuckled as he held out his hand to her mother. "It's good to meet you, but I'm afraid I'm a bit more than that. Betsy and I have been spending a lot of time together."

She adjusted her glasses. "You've been courting my daughter?"

It took August a minute, but it was now painfully obvious that Mrs. Detweiler was not a fan of his. Not even a little bit.

"Jah, I have." Feeling the ice of her glare, he swallowed. "Not formally, of course." And now he could feel the weight of Betsy's stare. "I admire Betsy very much."

When he glanced her way, August noticed that her expression was once again filled with compassion and warmth. It was obvious that she also thought her mother was being rather difficult.

"To what end?" Mrs. Detweiler asked.

When he faced her again, he wished he wouldn't have. She was looking like he was something ugly she'd found attached to her daughter's shoe. "I'm sorry?"

"If you admire my daughter so much and you are almost formally courting her . . . what do you hope to do?"

Do? What was she talking about? Sometimes, spending the majority of his life overseas created gaps in his understanding of common phrases and colloquialisms. Was she thinking he had something bad in mind?

"Mother, stop," Betsy interjected. "You're making both August and me uncomfortable."

"I only asked a simple question, which you still have not answered, young man." She sighed. "What's your real name, anyway?"

Things were going from bad to worse. Especially since Betsy's father had just entered the room.

"Hi, I'm Mark Detweiler, Betsy's father.

I'm guessing you're the young man Betsy has been telling us about?"

"Jah." He walked to the door and shook his hand. "I hope I am," he said with a smile. "It's gut to meet you. I'm August Troyer."

"I just asked him what his real name was," Mrs. Detweiler said.

Betsy groaned. "Mother, I have no idea what you are doing, but I wish you'd stop. Right away."

"I'm not doing anything. All I did was ask a simple question." She folded her arms across her chest as she studied him again. "Why aren't you answering what I ask?"

"Well, um, Betsy might have told you that I grew up all over the world because my parents are missionaries. Sometimes I don't always understand things right away."

"All I asked was your name."

"It's August."

"I mean your real name. If your parents are so devout that they're missionaries, I'm sure they didn't name you after a month of the year. What did they name you at birth?"

Mr. Detweiler placed a hand on his wife's arm. "Fawn, I know you're upset, but you're out of line."

"I don't mind answering. Mrs. Detweiler, my parents named me August at birth, I'm afraid. It is my real name. I was born in August, you see." He felt a bit idiotic pointing that out, but what could he do?

"Oh." She looked taken aback.

"They were not ones to put on airs about names and such. My father always liked the name and they decided that the Lord liked it too, since I was born a week later than expected, on August second." And . . . now he had not only shared his birthday but given them way more information than they probably ever wanted to know.

To his surprise, Mr. Detweiler grinned. "Your parents sound like my sort of people. I like that they take things as they come."

August exhaled. "They are good people."

"I like your name too," Betsy whispered.

"Danke."

"You still haven't told us about your plans for the two of you."

"Mamm, we only just met. August has been teaching me to play golf and we've shared some meals together. Don't make our friendship out to be something sneaky and devious."

When her mother's expression tightened but she didn't say anything else, August decided that he should probably leave. As much as he wanted to spend time with Betsy and make sure she knew that he was concerned about her, he didn't want to be grilled by her mother anymore.

Turning toward Betsy, he reached for her hand again. "I think that I should probably leave. When will you be getting discharged?"

"I'm not sure, but hopefully in the next day or so."

"Will you be staying at Mary and Jayson's haus again?"

Betsy glanced nervously at her parents. "I hope so. We were just discussing this before you got here."

"Will you either come by the golf shop or send word about where you'll be so I can see you?" August hated to be pushy, but he was starting to feel like he needed to make sure that she didn't forget to let him know what was going on.

"Of course I will," she said softly.

"Danke. I hope you feel better soon."

"Thank you for coming to see me."

"Of course. There was nowhere else I wanted to be." Steeling his shoulders, he turned to her parents. "Though I'm sorry about the circumstances, it was good to meet you."

"We are pleased to meet you too," Mrs. Detweiler said.

Mr. Detweiler shook August's hand.

"Hopefully we'll see you again before we leave."

"I hope so." Of course, that was a bit of a fib. He would actually be very fine if he didn't see them again.

Just before he walked out the door, he caught Betsy's eye. She was looking at him like there was so much she wished she could say.

He sent her a sympathetic smile as he walked out. Betsy had her hands full with them and he felt sorry for her. But as he went down the elevator, he felt burdened too. Betsy's illness, his father's injury, and his mother's request that he leave everything in Pinecraft in order to become a missionary were heavy on his mind. He'd always believed that the Lord never gave a person more weight than they could bear.

Unfortunately, but it was feeling almost like too much at the moment. Especially since he had no idea how to make things lighter.

23

Feeling shaken, Annie set down her phone as she went to find Danielle. She found her in the pool, swimming laps. Music was playing through a pair of speakers. As worried as she was, Danny's choice of tunes made her chuckle — it was old eighties and nineties rock and roll. If Annie wasn't mistaken, her sister must have swum to the songs more than a time or two. Each stroke was in sync with the beat.

As Annie stood on the side and watched Danielle execute a flip turn, she wondered what her niece and nephew would think if they could see her right now. They were sure their mother only cared about being fancy and acting refined. Annie was pretty certain that they would be shocked to discover that Danielle likely knew every word to an Aerosmith power ballad.

Since Annie had never attempted to be fancy or refined, she sat down on the side of the pool, stuck her feet in the water, and sang the chorus to "I Don't Want to Miss a Thing."

When Danielle paused for a break, she laughed. "Listen to you singing!"

"I couldn't help it; I always loved this song, even though I still can't sing a single note on key."

"Me neither. We're hopeless. No wonder neither of us liked choir."

Annie groaned. "Don't remind me. I barely got out of there with a B."

"You did better than me. Remember how I used to skip and get in so much trouble?"

Sharing a smile with Danielle, Annie chuckled. "Mom and Dad were so mad. Every single time."

Danielle rested her elbows on the side. "I never was too good at learning from my mistakes." As Aerosmith's song faded, she looked around. "Where's Betsy? Is she in the bathroom getting changed?"

"No. Her friend Mary called." She drew in a breath. "Betsy's in the hospital."

"What?"

Danielle's slack expression mimicked how she was feeling. "I couldn't believe it either. Mary said she had an asthma attack of some sort the other night. An ambulance had to come get her."

"Oh no! Is she going to be okay?"

"I think so, but she's going to be in the hospital at least another night," she replied as she got back on her feet.

Danielle pulled herself out of the pool and perched on the ledge. "You know what, she did act like she was having a harder time swimming during her last lesson. I put it down to the fact that she needed to get in swim shape." She frowned. "Annie, do you think I pushed her too hard? Is it my fault she's there?"

"If it's your fault, it's my fault too." Annie thought about the last lesson for a moment, then shook her head. "I don't think this was our doing. I mean, I hope not." Noticing that her sister continued to look guilty, she added, "Danny, I promise that I thought the same thing you did. Every swimmer gets out of breath whenever they haven't swum in a while, or if they're trying to get stronger. It happens to me every time."

"It happens for me too. I wish I would've asked Betsy more questions about her asthma, though."

"Hey, what do you think about visiting Betsy in the hospital? I remember a couple of years ago when I had surgery, I hated sitting in that room. I'm sure she's lonely."

Danielle brightened. "I think that's a great

idea. I was just about to suggest it to you. We could get her some flowers and magazines or something." She frowned. "Do you think that she's allowed to read them? I don't want to inadvertently offend her."

"I don't know if Amish ladies are allowed to read magazines or not, but I say let's get them. She's got to be bored."

"That sounds like a plan. If Betsy doesn't want them, then we'll take them back home. She doesn't seem like the type to not tell us if she's uncomfortable."

Annie nodded. "I agree."

Danielle got to her feet and walked to one of the tables on the patio to get a towel. "Can you be ready in thirty minutes?"

"I can, but can you?"

"Absolutely."

"Really?"

"Really, Annie. One of the reasons I used to always take a really long time getting ready was because Peter kept me on edge. If I wasn't put together, he let me know it."

Once again Annie wished she wouldn't have taken everything that Peter said at face value. "I'm sorry I never asked more questions about how you were feeling, Danny. I really regret that."

Danielle's bottom lip trembled before she visibly reined in her emotions. "Nope. We're not going down that path right now. We've got a sweet, gorgeous Amish girl to cheer up. What do you think about chocolate?"

Annie chuckled as she hurried to her room. "I think everyone likes chocolate, whether they're Amish, English, or anything else," she said over her shoulder. "I'll see you in thirty minutes."

Ninety minutes after Annie told Danielle the news, the two of them were walking down the hall to visit Betsy with way too much stuff in their hands. Not only had they picked up chocolate, magazines, and flowers, they'd gotten her cute socks, a fluffy robe, hand lotion, and a book of crossword puzzles and word searches. And a really big purple and pink balloon that proclaimed "Get Well Soon" in yellow letters.

The balloon, of course, had been Danielle's idea, but Annie had happily gone along with it. Betsy was a darling girl and possessed quite a bit of spunk. She was pretty sure that Betsy would be both amused and touched by the grand gesture.

When they got to her door, they peeked through the door's window. Annie discovered Betsy was definitely there, but she looked so small and alone in the hospital bed. She also looked pale, and her hair was in a neat braid but her kapp was off. She had an IV and two other monitors attached to her body. The sight of it all broke Annie's heart. "Poor little thing."

"It's so good we came, Annie," Danielle whispered before they walked in after two quick raps on the door.

Betsy gaped when she spied them. "What are you two doing here?"

"Visiting you, silly," Danielle said as she walked to her side. "We missed you!"

"Danielle's right," Annie added as she joined her sister at the side of Betsy's bed. "The two of us got to talking and decided that we simply can't go a week without seeing you. You're stuck with us now."

"Unfortunately, I'm not going to be able to swim too good in here," Betsy joked.

Annie felt some of the worry she'd been feeling about the girl ease a bit. If Betsy could make jokes, it was a sure sign that she was going to recover.

Danielle handed her their gift bag. "It's just as well that you can't swim. You've got other things to do right now."

Betsy grinned at the obnoxious balloon still clutched in Annie's hand. "And look at, as well."

"Do you like the balloon?"

"I do. I like the flowers too. You didn't

242

have to go to all this trouble, though."

"It's no trouble to care about you, Betsy," Annie said as she stepped closer to the small desk located under the window. "What do you think about me tying this balloon to one of the table legs over here?"

"I think that it would be a good spot."

Annie tied the balloon in a bow so either Betsy or a nurse could easily remove it and placed the flowers on the table.

When she returned to Danielle's side, she noticed that Danielle had pulled over some chairs for them to sit in.

Betsy was still holding the gift bag on her lap, almost like she didn't know what to do with it. "This is heavy."

Danielle frowned. "Is it too much for you to deal with? I can help you hold it, if you'd like."

"Nee. It's not that at all. It's j-just that . . ." Her voice drifted off as she visibly pulled herself together. "It's just that I still canna believe that you two came to see me at the hospital. How did you know I was even in here?"

"Your friend Mary Margaret told us," Annie said gently. "The minute I got off the phone, I told Danielle."

Danielle smiled. "And a couple minutes after that, we started making plans to visit."

"Y-you two didn't have to come here, you know."

"We wanted to, sweetie," Danielle said. "We're friends now, right?"

At last, a smile lit Betsy's face. "Jah. We are."

"Then go ahead and open the bag!" Annie said, hoping to lighten the girl's spirits since the last thing they'd wanted to do was make her upset. "I can't wait until you see everything we got you."

Danielle chuckled. "Be warned, though. I'm afraid we went a little crazy at the mall."

Betsy giggled as she pulled out the bright polka-dotted tissue paper and tossed it on top of her blanket, then spilled the entire contents on her lap.

And there it all was. Magazines, Life Savers, lotion, socks, crossword puzzles, word finds, a devotional, and four bars of chocolate.

Immediately, she picked up a bar of chocolate. "Oh, yum, I love this kind."

Danielle burst out laughing. "Annie and I both said that every woman needs a bar of chocolate from time to time."

Still smiling, Betsy picked up the magazines and the puzzle books and even unscrewed the top of the lotion and smelled inside. "I love everything. Thank you both so much."

"Are the magazines okay? You won't get in trouble, will you?" Annie asked.

Betsy frowned. "Why would I get in trouble?"

"You know, because you're Amish?"

"We weren't sure if there were certain magazines you shouldn't see and maybe someone would get upset with you if they saw you with one," Danielle added.

Betsy giggled. "Oh nee. I promise, there's no Amish police lurking around the hospital's halls."

The three of them had just burst out laughing when Betsy's room door opened again. Annie glanced over her shoulder, prepared to get out of the way for a nurse but saw an Amish couple instead. The woman looked like an older version of Betsy. The man had a dark brown beard and matching eyes. However, neither looked all that pleased to see them.

"You have more visitors, Betsy?" the man said. "I had no idea you made so many friends while you were here."

As Danielle and Annie stood up, some of the happy excitement in Betsy's expression faded.

"Mamm, Daed, this is Danielle and Annie. Danielle has been teaching me how to

swim. Annie is her sister and has been helping me too."

"I try to make sure Betsy doesn't drown,"
Annie joked.

It was immediately apparent her quip did
not go over well.

After a few seconds passed, Betsy added,
"They're really nice ladies."

"Can you swim now, Betsy?" her father
asked.

"K-kind of."

Like an avenging angel, Danielle reached
for Betsy's hand. "Hey, what did we talk
about? Do you remember?"

"That I can do anything I put my mind
to," Betsy whispered.

"That's right. And you can definitely
swim. I have no worries about you swimming from one end of the pool to the other."

Twin spots of color appeared on Betsy's
cheeks. "That is true. My breaststroke isn't
pretty, but I can do it." She lifted her chin.
"Yes, I can swim."

Annie had to chime in. "We're so proud
of you, honey. You were scared, but you
conquered your fears!"

"I couldn't have done it without you
both."

Betsy's mother cleared her throat. "I
didn't realize all what you've been doing,

daughter."

"You did know, Mamm. I told you."

"Jah, but to hear it like this . . ." Her voice drifted off. "These women are right. You have a lot to be proud about."

"Danke, Mamm."

"Now, what is all of this on the bed?" Betsy's father asked. He walked over and picked up one of the magazines — a *Better Homes and Gardens* — and thumbed through the pages. Turning to Annie and Danielle, he said, "You brought her magazines?"

"Yes," Annie said.

When Betsy's father didn't say anything, Danielle blurted, "I'm sorry if she's not supposed to read them. It's just so . . . so boring sitting in the hospital. I promise, we tried not to get Betsy anything too bad."

He held up the magazine. "You don't think this is bad?"

Annie felt her cheeks heat. "No," she squeaked.

He stared at her a long moment, then grinned. "Ain't no telling what you would think of *Cosmo* then."

It took a bit for her to realize that he was referring to *Cosmopolitan* magazine. And another few seconds to realize he was giving her a hard time on purpose.

She burst out laughing. Then Danny and Betsy did too. Soon, Betsy's parents were chuckling as well.

Smiling at Betsy, Annie said, "I'm so glad we met on the SCAT."

"Me too," Betsy replied. "You two have been a blessing to me."

Annie would say the same thing about Betsy.

24

Nate was his best friend. They'd met on the golf course, and the way Nate had accepted him — just a couple weeks after he'd moved to Pinecraft — was something August would always be grateful for. Nate had never made fun of some of the things August used to do. He'd had a few quirks from living the majority of his life in other countries around the world. But instead of teasing him, Nate had either accepted the quirks or recommended a better way to do or say things.

So, Nate was a really good friend, and a person August was usually glad to see whenever he wandered into the pro shop. Just not that day.

The problem was that Nate was in a good mood. A *really* good mood. It was hard to take, given that August was currently feeling like his whole world was falling apart.

He tried to hide his irritation by putting the new order of score cards in a container on the counter while Nate chattered like a magpie.

"I couldn't believe it, but Brianna's mamm actually sat down and visited with me for a couple of minutes before Brianna came into their living room. I really think she's beginning to like me," Nate said. "And guess what?"

He lifted his head. "What?"

"We didn't have a chaperone this time. Tonya wasn't anywhere to be found. It was awesome."

"That's nice." He opened up a box of pencils and added them to the plastic container next to the score cards.

Nate was grinning like a fool. August was pretty sure he would've been acting the same way if he was his buddy. It was just too bad that Nate was about to have his wishes and prayers answered while most of August's were still being ignored.

Of course, August knew his assessment wasn't fair or accurate. He also wasn't proud of himself for even thinking such selfish thoughts. However, if he had learned anything in life, it was that the Lord didn't expect him to be perfect or always at his best. God valued him even when he was at his worst.

Summoning a bit more enthusiasm, he

added, "I'm happy for you."

"Danke, but you don't sound all that happy, August. As a matter of fact, you look as glum as if you're about to get a tooth pulled."

"Don't worry about it." He pulled out a package of mini calendars to put in the third container.

"Stop with the organizing and tell me what's really wrong."

August tossed the package on the counter. "Fine. Look, I'm sorry that I don't seem happier for you. I promise that I really am."

"Okay . . ."

"It's just that I've gotten some awful news and I'm not sure what to do." Or, rather, he knew what he should do . . . he just didn't want to.

Nate stared at him in concern. "Is Betsy still in the hospital? Did she get worse?"

"Nee. Betsy is still there, but I think she's on the mend. She's going to be all right." He took off his hat and ran his fingers through his hair. "I heard from my mother again. She's still pushing me to book a plane flight."

"He's not getting any better?"

"It doesn't seem like it."

"Hey, I'm really sorry. What's going to happen? Are they going to fly him here to get better treatment?"

"Nee. I'm afraid my father would consider leaving the country for treatment as giving up." August shrugged. "Though I don't exactly agree, I can see his point of view."

Nate's expression became even more concerned. "I'll pray for him — and for you and your family."

"Danke. I appreciate your prayers, but I'm afraid that my father's health isn't the only thing on my mind. I still don't want to go, but I feel guilty. Shouldn't I want to do anything I can to help?"

"You can love your father and worry about his health without doing a job that doesn't suit you. Mission work ain't your calling."

"You're right. It isn't. I even feel like me being there wouldn't be a blessing to the villagers they're working with. I don't know anyone there, and I'm not even exactly sure what they're working on."

"You'd simply be a warm body giving a hand."

"Jah. Or getting in the way," August said. "But that's not how they see things. All they see is that I'm their son, they're my parents, and they want me to step up."

Nate shook his head. "That's not stepping up, though. Forgive me, but I think if you do as your mother asks, you'll be preventing someone who does have a heart for missionary work to go. Plus, you already are doing your part. You have a good job and you work hard at it. Your parents are only thinking about their needs. They're wanting you to leave everything you have here."

"I know."

Nate waved a hand. "And what about Gideon and Diane? They count on you. You run this place. I know they have a couple of teenagers helping out, but they surely can't take your place. You do everything around here."

It was such a relief to hear Nate verbalize some of the same things that he'd been thinking. "I know that too."

"And what about Betsy? You and her are getting close, August," Nate continued, obviously on a roll. "I've seen you two together. She really likes you. Anyone can see that. She's going to be so upset if you leave for Africa. Plus, she's in the hospital! You canna just up and leave her right now. That wouldn't be right at all."

Nate's staunch support and irritation on his behalf almost made him smile. "I feel the same way, but I don't know if I have a choice."

"Of course you do . . . unless you've already made your decision?"

"I haven't made anything close to a decision. Actually, I haven't done anything but either feel so guilty I can hardly think . . . or fume and worry." He waved a hand. "And now, here I am, complaining to you."

"Complain all you want. That's what friends are for, ain't so?"

"Yeah." They shared a smile before August sobered again. "I feel like I need to go to Africa, Nate. My mother asked, and she doesn't ask me to do very much."

Nate studied him for a long minute. It was almost as if he was debating about whether to speak his mind.

August knew if their positions were reversed, he would do the same. Their friendship was solid, and it was based not only on a love of golf but on shared values and genuine respect for each other. But sometimes a person didn't need tentative platitudes or vague opinions. Sometimes only blunt words helped. This was one of those times.

"Just say it, Nate."

"All right." He stuffed his hands in his pockets, like he was bracing himself. "Here goes. I know you love your parents, but I think you're mixing up guilt and obligation with what they're asking you to do."

Looking even more intent, he added,

254

"Your mother might not ask much of you, but she doesn't give you much, either. Time and again you've shared how difficult those Skype calls are for you — because they don't seem to care about your job or your life here. All they ever do is make you feel guilty for not following in their footsteps."

Nate took a deep breath and continued. "Furthermore, I think their request sounds selfish. Instead of admitting that another experienced missionary needs to come and take over, they want to stay and bring you in. Your mother and father don't want to have to admit that other people could do a better job for the people they're trying to help."

"Wow, Nate." He'd expected honesty, but this was brutal honesty.

Nate's cheeks flushed. "I'm sorry if I said too much. Obviously, you don't have to pay me any mind."

August clasped his arm. "You didn't say too much. I wanted to hear what you really thought, and I'm glad you said what you did."

"Did I help at all?"

"Honestly, nee. But you have given me a lot to think about."

"So, when do you have to make a decision?"

"Soon." Grimacing, he added, "Yesterday." He knew his mother was hoping he'd be on a plane headed their way within a couple of days.

"I hope you'll take as much time as you need to think about this, August. It's a really big decision."

"I'm going to pray some more. The Lord already knows how I feel — and what my parents and the people in their mission need." Meeting Nate's gaze again, he said, "I just hope that He'll tell me what to do in a pretty bold way. I need an answer, not just a hint."

Nate chuckled. "You might be waiting a long time for that. Our Lord is everything, but He ain't one for conveying His wishes real clearly."

"He works miracles, though . . . so maybe He'll decide to tell me exactly what to do."

"I hope you're right," Nate said.

August did too.

25

She was still in the hospital, she was still getting poked and prodded, and her parents were still driving her crazy. As much as she wanted to be in a better mood and give Liza, the poor nurse assigned to her, a break, Betsy didn't know if it was possible.

"Blow into the tube one more time, Betsy," Liza said.

Dutifully, Betsy took a deep breath, placed her lips around the cardboard tube, and exhaled with as much force as she could.

Unfortunately, even she knew the result wasn't very good.

Liza looked at the reading on the monitor, blinked, and then asked, "Are you pressing your lips firmly around the tube? If you don't, some of the air will escape."

Oh, she knew. Betsy had been doing this test to gauge lung capacity for years. "I am. No air is escaping."

"I see." Liza ran her fingers along the

electronic screen, stared at it intently, then finally handed her another cardboard tube. "Let's do this again, please."

Betsy didn't want to. She was tired of being poked and prodded, tired of being woken up in the middle of the night, and tired of doing just about everything they had asked her to do for the last three days.

But most of all, she was tired of taking this stupid lung capacity test and failing it.

Betsy wanted to fold her arms over her chest and tell Liza no. But she wouldn't. Betsy wasn't the kind of woman to throw a fit in a hospital. So, of course she wouldn't act horrible.

But there was another reason, as well.

She wasn't going to refuse to do the test because it wouldn't change a thing. She would still have to take the test as many times as she was asked. She was trapped here until she got better.

She held out her hand, waited for the nurse to set up the machine again, and then helped her hold the tube to her lips. Then, just like the million times before, she inhaled as best she could, covered the stupid piece of cardboard with her lips, and exhaled.

When she was done, she leaned back against her chair and attempted to catch her breath. She didn't even try to hide her exhaustion or her pain. She was tired and her lungs hurt.

Liza's expression softened. "All right. Let's see what this says."

Betsy closed her eyes. She wasn't eager to see either the numbers or the nurse's expression when she read the dismal reading.

"Betsy, are you all right?" Liza sounded a little panicked.

"Jah. I'm just tired."

"Are you sure? How do you feel? How are your lungs feeling?"

She opened one eye. "Not too good."

"Give me a number."

Betsy shrugged. "Maybe a seven on the pain scale?"

The nurse looked even more concerned. "Do they feel sore or are they burning?"

"My lungs are only sore, Liza. That's all."

After making a notation on her clipboard, Liza stood up. "All right. Let's get you back in bed, sweetie. Would you like a warm blanket?"

"Yes, please." The blankets that they kept in warming bins were heavenly and would feel so good.

"I'll be right back with one." Liza poured some ice water into a plastic glass. "Sip some water for me, okay? Try to drink it all."

As she watched the nurse wheel out the machine, Betsy sipped her water. The minute she was all alone, she released a ragged sigh. The truth was that she was worried. She was in a bad way this time. Her expected twenty-four-hour stay had lingered to three days. If she didn't get better fast, then it might stretch to four. She really didn't want to be in the hospital for another full day and night.

Liza entered again with the promised blanket in her hands. "Here you go, dear. Would you like some more water? Maybe apple juice?"

"Thank you, but nee." She was getting so sleepy.

"All right. Why don't you rest for a bit? I left a message for Dr. Klimek. I have a feeling he'll be by later this afternoon."

Betsy nodded. Cuddling under the blanket, she let her eyes drift closed. She was so tired. As her body turned heavy, she knew sleep was on the way. She was grateful for that. At least she wouldn't have to worry about having to breathe into another tube for a while.

Two hours later, the first thing Betsy was aware of was that someone was holding her hand. The second was that August was the one doing so.

"Ah. There you are," he said with a smile. "I was starting to wonder if you were ever going to wake up."

"What are you doing in here?"

"I came to pay you a visit. When I saw you were sound asleep, I decided to sit with you while you slept." He winked. "I'm pleased to tell you that you didn't make a peep. Not one snore."

She smiled. "I didn't think I snored. I'm glad I was right. So, um, why did you sit here and watch me sleep? It sounds pretty boring to me."

"First of all, it wasn't boring. I was actually glad to have a reason to sit and relax in the quiet." He leaned closer. Close enough to catch a hint of the familiar-smelling soap he favored. "Secondly, I stayed because I wanted to be with you. I'm worried about you, Betsy."

Becoming more awake, Betsy pressed the button on the bed so she could sit up. And then, of course, she was acutely aware that she was sitting in a nightgown and no doubt looked horrible. She pulled the blanket up more securely around her. "There's no need to worry," she finally said. "I'm all right."

"That's good to hear." He handed her the plastic glass. "Here you go. The nice nurse who escorted me here told me to make sure you drank more water when you woke up."

Thirsty, she took the glass gratefully and drank almost the whole contents. "Danke."

"Of course." He took the cup and filled it again. "Would you like some more?"

"Thanks, but I'm okay for now." August's presence made her wonder where her parents were. "Have you seen my mamm and daed?"

He smiled. "I have. They came in about a half an hour ago. Since I was here, they said they were going to go have some lunch."

She was shocked. "They left you alone with me?"

He frowned. "Were they not supposed to? Do you need them?" He moved to stand up. "Hey, maybe —"

"Nee, it's not that. It's more the fact that my parents left at all. They usually camp out in here even if I'm sleeping. I'm surprised, that's all." She was also surprised that they left him alone with her.

"We had a nice conversation. Your parents seemed, ah, a lot nicer this time."

Thinking that her mother, especially, could have only acted better than the last time she'd seen August, Betsy smiled. "I'm really glad to hear that. As you know, they can be overwhelming at times. Especially when I'm sick."

"I can't blame them for that. I'm worried, and you're not my daughter."

"Overall, they're wonderful to be around."

"Then you're blessed."

"Are your parents not like that?"

"Not exactly."

She noticed then that August seemed not only concerned about her but worried in general. "Hey, what's wrong?"

"It's nothing that you need to be worrying about."

"I'm sorry, but I'd love to worry about someone other than myself." She tried again. "August, talk to me, please. What's going on? What's troubling you?"

"My mother wants me to move to Africa."

Stunned, she gaped. "When do they want you to go? And why?"

He shifted in his chair. "Well, soon. My father hurt his leg and had to have surgery. Now he has a bad infection."

"I'm so sorry." She knew enough about the different infections floating around hospitals to realize that his father's situation could be really serious. "I hope he'll get better soon."

"I do too, but I don't know." He sighed. "Betsy, they want me to help out at the mission."

She had a lot to say about that, but she supposed it didn't matter. "Are you going to do it?"

"I actually came over here to talk to you about it. But now I realize that was really selfish." Looking irritated with himself, he added, "Just like my even mentioning this to you right now was selfish. I'm sorry."

"August, just because I'm stuck in here doesn't mean that I'm not interested in other things. I want to know about what you're dealing with."

He rubbed the knuckles of her hand with his thumb, startling her. She'd been so comfortable with him that she'd forgotten they were holding hands. "Betsy, I'm feeling torn. I feel like I should do what my parents want, but I also want to be my own man."

"Have you been praying?"

"I have."

"What has the Lord told you?"

August rolled his eyes. "Unfortunately, He's been pretty silent on the matter."

She gave him a sympathetic look. "I've had a couple of those moments myself."

"Any advice?"

"Jah. Listen harder." Smiling slightly, she lowered her voice. "Sometimes God decides to whisper."

When he grinned, Betsy realized that God

had been whispering in her ear too. She just hadn't been listening. She needed to rectify that as soon as possible.

26

It was late afternoon when August stepped through the hospital's automatic sliding glass doors. As always, getting used to the change in temperatures took a moment. He reckoned the temperature in the hospital had been right at seventy degrees while the humid, late afternoon heat had to be near one hundred.

He didn't mind taking some time to get acclimated, since he had a feeling it was going to take him a whole lot longer to come to terms with everything that had happened during the last three hours.

All in all, it had been a pretty strange visit at the hospital. Or maybe it had been so filled with unexpected moments that he was still attempting to wrap his head around them all. Not only had he felt compelled to sit in Betsy's room while she'd been sleeping, but he hadn't even offered to leave when her parents first arrived.

Then, after Betsy had woken up, he'd continued to hold her hand. He might have started holding it for her sake — so she wouldn't feel so alone — but it had become clear to him that he'd stayed where he was as much for himself as for her. August liked being linked with her. Even when she was asleep, Betsy calmed him.

But by far the most surprising moment had been when the doctor and her parents arrived at the same time and Betsy asked him to stay nearby. He left the room with her parents when she was being examined but was brought in when the doctor said that she was well enough to leave the hospital but not well enough to travel.

When Dr. Klimek looked August in the eye and asked if he would be able to help watch over Betsy, August answered without hesitation.

He promised he would be there.

It was as if another person was in charge of his mouth — since he was pretty sure he was still wrestling with his decision about Africa.

When the sliding doors opened again, Mark Detweiler strode out. "August, I'm so glad I found you. I told Fawn that it was a longshot, but here you are."

"I was just, um, getting my bearings. Is

something wrong? Do you need something?"

"I do, but I'm hoping for a moment of your time, not anything in particular." Seeing the SCAT approach, Mr. Detweiler winced slightly. "I hate to do this to you, since it means you'll miss your ride, but could we talk? Please?"

There was a part of him that wanted to refuse. Missing this bus meant he likely wouldn't get back to the golf course for at least another two hours. But, of course, there was no way he would refuse. "All right," he said, though a hint of foreboding filled him.

He really hoped Mr. Detweiler wasn't about to tell him to stay away from Betsy. As far as August was concerned, he hadn't done a thing for Betsy's parents to be upset about. But that didn't mean that they were going to accept him into their daughter's life.

"Danke. I really appreciate it."

August was growing more concerned. "Do you want to go back inside?"

"Nee, being outside is a nice change from the cold air-conditioning. However, I would like to stay close." Looking around the area, he gestured to a dark green metal picnic table set just to their left. "Do you mind if we sit down over there?"

"Of course not. That's fine." The area was obviously used for hospital personnel or visitors in need of a place to relax. At the moment, it was completely empty.

The picnic table was under a collection of palm trees. The setting provided not only some shade but a little feeling of whimsy to the hospital grounds. August could imagine more than one visitor gazing up at the palm fronds and feeling a little bit of stress melt away.

"I know you're a busy man, so I'll get right to the point," Mr. Detweiler said. "I . . . that is, Fawn and I . . . well, we wanted to thank you for everything you've done for our daughter."

"You're welcome, but I haven't done anything special. I wanted to visit her here."

"I'm not just talking about today, August. I'm talking about being here for Betsy the whole time she's been here."

"We've become close." He thought that was obvious, but he was still missing the man's point. "It's been everything proper, though. I promise you that."

"I understand." Mr. Detweiler looked down at his hands, which were clasped together on the table. "I'm gonna be honest. When I first saw you holding Betsy's hand, I wasn't happy."

"I got that impression," August said in a dry tone.

Mr. Detweiler's eyes lit up as humor filled his gaze. "Obviously Fawn wasn't either." He chuckled softly. "When we first walked out of Betsy's room, we were figuring out how to get you out of there . . . until a nice nurse stopped us in the hall and mentioned how it was so obvious that you care about her."

He shifted. "You see, August, my wife and I realized that we've been doing Betsy a disservice. We started thinking that because she has had problems with her lungs, that she has different wants and needs than other women her age. But that's not the case. She has every right to want to do things, make friends . . . and have a boyfriend. We realized that all our efforts to protect her hadn't been as much for her as for us."

August completely agreed, but he wasn't sure why Betsy's father had hurried outside to tell him all that. "I'm, ah, glad you came to that conclusion."

"I am too. We shouldn't have let all the memories of almost losing her taint everything else."

"I can only imagine seeing your daughter struggle to breathe would be impossible to ever forget." He hadn't liked seeing her having to use an inhaler on the golf course.

"Anyway, I wanted to thank you for helping to open our eyes and also to apologize for our rudeness. It wasn't right, and I know we embarrassed Betsy."

At least he knew what to say now. "There's no need to worry about me. I've learned that one doesn't always act their best in a difficult situation. Sometimes, when people are really stressed, they say and do things they might not if they were in a calmer situation. I saw that time and again when my parents and I lived in some countries recovering from a natural disaster."

"Ah yes. Betsy said your parents were missionaries."

He nodded. "Once, when we were living in Haiti, there was so much devastation, heartache, and pain. Many people were simply trying to get clean water — they weren't even hoping for something to eat or shelter. At first I was shocked because some of the men and women didn't act all that grateful, but then my parents reminded me that it was wrong to judge someone unless I'd walked in their shoes." He shrugged. "My father's words have always stayed with me."

A new respect entered Mr. Detweiler's

expression. "Your father sounds like a wise man."

"He is. He is a wise man." August felt a lump form in his throat. As much as he didn't get along with them, he couldn't deny that they'd done a lot of good in their lives. Had he been so focused on their imperfections that he'd forgotten everything that was commendable about them?

Mr. Detweiler cleared his throat. "I don't want to take up much more of your time. I just wanted to try to make things better between us. I don't want you to think that we're going to sabotage your relationship or anything."

"I'm glad you wanted to talk." Thinking of Betsy, he added, "I'm sure she'll be glad we talked too."

Mr. Detweiler chuckled. "You know Betsy. She might look demure, but she's not that way at all. She doesn't shy away from telling us when she thinks we're wrong about something."

"I've learned that too."

Mr. Detweiler stood up. "Listen, I don't know what's going to happen with you and Betsy. Our daughter reminded us that relationships don't involve four people, just two. But, um, if things do happen to move forward between the two of you? I wanted you to know that you'll have nothing but Fawn's and my support. You make Betsy happy and seem to appreciate not just her beauty and sweet disposition but also her spunk and the light that always seems to shine around her."

"I appreciate you saying that." August couldn't help it, he burst out laughing. "If she's this spunky now, I can only imagine how she was when she was younger."

Mr. Detweiler pointed to his dark hair that was liberally sprinkled with gray. "I'm pretty sure she's given me every one of these gray strands."

August smiled as he held out his hand. "I'll check in tomorrow. Betsy has the golf course's phone number. Please remind her to call me if she gets released?" Sobering, he added, "Or if something happens, would you or Mrs. Detweiler please let me know?"

"Of course," Mr. Detweiler said as they shook hands. "God be with you, August."

"With you as well."

They parted ways, Mr. Detweiler walking back through the sliding doors and August back to the SCAT stop. After glancing at the schedule, he noticed that the next bus that would stop in Pinecraft wasn't scheduled to arrive for almost forty-five minutes.

Remembering something that his mother

used to say, that God gave him perfectly good feet, he decided to start walking back home. It might take a while, but he had a lot to think about. Both about Mr. Detweiler's words, his feelings for Betsy, and his parents in Africa.

It was time he made some decisions.

27

At long last, Annie was finally going out on a date with Jack. They'd had to reschedule twice. Once because of Jack's work and once because Annie had been so worried about Betsy and thought she might need something.

Annie met Jack at The Boardwalk, a funky, high-end bistro just outside of the Pinecraft section of Sarasota. She and Danielle had discovered it one evening and had instantly become huge fans of the food, the restaurant's ambiance . . . and a waiter named Michael.

They'd soon learned that Michael was also the assistant manager of the restaurant. Though he seemed awfully young for that much responsibility, Annie couldn't deny that he did a great job. He was not only efficient, but he was personable and handsome. He had the prettiest wife too. Another one of the servers had told them that Michael and his wife, Esther, were newlyweds. Annie and Danielle had thought they were adorable. It was so nice to see a couple completely in love.

Feeling terrible that she'd had to postpone their makeup lunch date, Annie invited Jack to meet her at The Boardwalk for dinner. Since she had a feeling that Jack would want to be the one to pay for their date, she decided to turn the tables. Annie was going to pay for dinner. She wanted to treat him to show how glad she was that he hadn't given up on her.

She'd just approached the hostess counter when Jack walked in. This time, instead of looking scruffy in shorts, flip-flops, and beach hair, he had shorter hair, tan slacks, and a teal-colored linen shirt.

"Jack, hi!"

"Hi." He grinned. "Is it rude to admit that I had to do a double take?"

She looked at her outfit. She was wearing a navy silk dress, three-inch heels, and makeup, and her curly hair was styled into soft waves. "It's not rude at all. As I got ready, it kind of occurred to me that you've only seen me at my worst."

"I thought you looked great on the beach." He lowered his voice. "You do look beautiful all dolled up, though."

She smiled at him as Kim, the manager, greeted them.

"Hi. It's Annie, right?"

"Yes. My friend Jack and I have dinner reservations."

"Thank you for coming in again. I see your name right here." She smiled as she looked at the printed sheet of paper on the podium. "I also see that you asked for a table by the windows. We have it ready for you."

As they followed Kim to the only empty table in the whole restaurant, she noticed that Jack looked impressed.

"You must either be a really good customer or you pulled some strings," he said. "This has to be one of the most popular restaurants in Sarasota. Not only did the local paper say it was difficult to get a reservation sooner than two weeks out, I spied the list of folks who were waiting for tables. There's got to be more than twenty names on it."

"I'm a good customer . . . and I might have done a little bit of begging," she teased as they sat down and received their menus.

"I hope you enjoy your dinner," Kim said before she walked away.

When they were alone, Jack looked out the window at the view. Though it was just a street view, there was a front courtyard in between them and the street. The owners of the restaurant had planted a profusion of flowers and shrubs. There were also several bird feeders in copper holders and hanging on black metal hooks. The courtyard muffled some of the outside noise and gave them a sense of dining in a garden.

"I've heard of this place but haven't tried to get in yet," Jack said. "It's really terrific."

His praise made her laugh. "You haven't tried the food yet."

"I'm sure I'll love everything. Everyone else's meals look good."

"I've tried a lot of the dishes. Danielle and I come here often."

Eventually, the server arrived. Annie was delighted to see that it was Michael. "Hi, Michael. I wasn't sure if you were working tonight or not."

"I've been working in the back in addition to the dining room tonight. I'm actually only in charge of a couple of tables." He grinned. "It looks like you decided to bring someone new." He handed them a basket of bread and butter.

"I did. Jack is visiting Sarasota too but hasn't had the pleasure of dining here yet."

"I hope it exceeds your expectations, Jack."

"It already has."

A few minutes later, Michael returned with their drink orders.

"How is Esther?" Annie asked.

Michael grinned. "Terrific. She's working over at the Marigold Inn but only about twenty-five hours a week now. She's happy to have some extra time to explore the area."

"Michael and Esther are newlyweds," Annie explained.

"Congratulations," Jack said.

"Danke. God blessed me with her. We're mighty happy." He pulled out a pad of paper. "Now, may I take your orders?"

After they told Michael what they wanted, he moved away, smoothly stopping at two other tables on his way back to the kitchen.

After Michael disappeared through the door, she sighed. "I'm going to miss this place when I'm back in Cincinnati. Almost as much as I'm going to miss living here."

"Me too. When my parents suggested we have our family reunion here, I have to admit I was skeptical. There seemed to be a lot more exciting destinations, you know?"

"I do."

"Now, though, I feel like this whole area suits me fine."

"When do you leave, Jack?"

"Nothing is set in stone, but probably next

week sometime. What about you?"

"Next Friday. Danielle has to give up the house. I'm sure the landlord already has it booked for the next person."

Jack took a sip of water. "Hey, Annie, is there anything keeping you in Cincinnati? If you blog, you can work anywhere, right?"

She nodded. "I can. Danielle is there, of course, but it's not like we see each other all the time." She wondered if things would be different now that they'd begun to mend their relationship. "What about you? Do you have to stay in Toledo?"

"I do." He shrugged. "But I also travel a lot."

"Maybe you'll have the opportunity to come down to Cincinnati."

"It's less than a four-hour drive. I bet I can manage it."

When their salads arrived, they both seemed relieved to concentrate on their food. Later, when their main courses came, things seemed even more distant between them.

Annie felt like as soon as they discussed the reality of their lives, some of the magic of the night had worn off.

Things got worse when the bill came and Jack insisted on paying it. Though she knew he was trying to be a gentleman, Annie felt like it was yet another sign that they weren't destined for a long-term relationship. He was wealthy, she was not. He had an important job, she didn't. None of that mattered when they were on vacation, but maybe when they were far apart, some of the sparks that had been flying between them might fizzle out.

After they walked out, Annie decided not to drag things out. "I'm so glad you could join me for dinner, Jack. Thank you for the meal."

He reached for her hand. "Annie, wait. What are you doing?"

"I'm telling you good night."

"Don't you want to go for a walk or something? We didn't have dessert. I bet there's an ice cream place nearby. Would you like that?"

"Jack, thanks, but . . ." She moved off to the side so they were away from most people who were walking on the sidewalk. "Maybe it's silly to start something between us."

"Why?"

"Well, for starters, we live in two different cities."

"First, it's two different cities in the same state, not across the country. Second, if we both want to continue to talk and see each other, we'll find a way to do that."

"Do you really think so?"

"Absolutely," he said as he squeezed her hand. "Look, I know we hardly know each other, but I'd still like to see you again. I'm willing to give this relationship a try. Annie, I mean it."

Gazing into his face, she saw raw emotion in his eyes. He wasn't just telling her what he thought she wanted to hear, he was being completely serious. "All right. If you're sure . . ."

He glanced at her lips, then pulled her close and kissed her. Right on the street. And it wasn't just a chaste peck on the lips.

No, it was the real deal. A kiss between two grown people who knew what they wanted. Passionate enough to make a few passersby giggle.

Passionate enough to make Annie gasp for breath when they parted at last.

"I'm sure," he said. "Do you understand?"

"Yes. I . . . I think I got that impression."

"Good. Now, I'm still not ready to tell you good night. Would you like some ice cream, because I would."

She felt so flustered, she wasn't even sure she'd be able to taste it. "Sure?"

Jack laughed. "Let's go get some, then."

Feeling her cheeks heat, Annie held his hand and walked down the sidewalk. They passed two Amish couples, a group of teenagers, and a couple at least ten years younger than them kissing in a dark corner.

Annie couldn't help but smile a little smugly. That couple might be a little younger, but they didn't have anything on her and Jack. Not one thing at all.

28

Nate had just kissed Brianna in a dark corner in the middle of Sarasota. It hadn't been anything too outrageous — just a quick peck on her lips. But it had still been wrong.

When he felt her tremble, he dropped the hand that he'd been holding and for good measure stepped another six inches away. What had he been thinking? Her parents were going to kill him, and it was nothing less than he deserved too.

"Brianna, please forgive me," he sputtered. "I didn't mean to do that."

Even in the dim light, it was obvious that she was upset. Her other hand, the hand that he hadn't just been claiming, was covering her mouth. Wasn't that a bad sign?

Down went that hand, right as something hard entered her eyes. "You . . . you didn't mean to kiss me?"

"Nee! I don't know what happened. One

minute we were eating ice cream, and then the next, kissing you just seemed like a really good idea." Of course, part of the problem had been him watching her lick that stupid ice cream cone. "I promise, it won't happen again." Not until they were married. Maybe on their honeymoon.

She blinked. "It won't?"

"Of course not. Brianna, I respect you. I don't want to do anything that will cause you to feel uncomfortable or um . . . not respected." And now he sounded like an idiot. He was impulsive, a public kisser, and an idiot.

She was likely going to bar him from Yoder's so she'd never have to see him again.

"Come on," he said. He reached out to press his hand on the small of her back, then decided that was too intimate a touch. He stuffed his hands in his pockets instead. "I better get you home."

"Now? But it's only half past eight. My parents won't be expecting me to be home for at least another hour."

"Maybe they'll be pleased that I brought you home early?"

Her eyes narrowed. "Why would my parents be pleased about that?"

Nate had no idea. Drawn in by her blue eyes yet again, he improvised. "Because it shows that I'm respecting you?"

"Bringing me home an hour early is respectful but kissing isn't?"

"Jah?"

"I see."

He was starting to see that he was making things worse, because the current conversation they were having was a nightmare.

A dating nightmare.

Nate knew he had to get his head back together or he was going to make things worse than they already were. Spying a park bench a block away, he said, "Come on. Let's go sit over there and talk."

Brianna didn't look all that happy, but she walked with him to the bench and sat down.

When he joined her, she folded her arms across her chest. He was suddenly really glad they were in the dark, because if she could see the panic that was no doubt etched on his face, she'd likely never speak to him again. Mentally, he started thinking of things to tell her. Things like how he was pretty smart but still did dumb things. Or that he'd be happy to take Tonya out with them on their next date so she'd feel suitably chaperoned.

"So —" he began.

She interrupted. "Nate, before you start talking, I'd like to go first."

"Okay?" His hands started to sweat.

She sat up a little straighter. "Nate, I think you need to know something. For, um, whatever reason, I haven't been courted before. You see, I was once rather plain."

"I doubt that."

She shook her head. "I'm not trying to spur a compliment out of you. I'm trying to tell you that my body took a long time to well . . . develop." She bit her bottom lip. "For a while, the only sign I had that my body even knew what puberty was . . . was a real bad case of acne. It wasn't pretty."

"Brianna, I don't care about that. I went through an awkward stage too. Everyone does."

"Maybe you did, maybe you didn't. What matters to me is that while no one was exactly mean, no boys gave me the time of day. When most of my childhood friends started receiving attention and such, we drifted apart. That's when I started working at Yoder's. I started back in the kitchen, washing dishes and chopping vegetables. One day they were shorthanded and asked me to waitress." Her chin lifted. "It turned out I did a pretty good job."

"You're an excellent waitress, Brianna."

"Oh, Nate. You are such a *good* person." She laughed slightly. "What I've been trying to tell you is that my unfortunate awkward stage finally ended, and I did receive some attention. More than one boy asked me out. I said no to everyone."

"Why?" He was completely engrossed.

She shifted so they faced each other. "Because, by then, I had met you."

"At the restaurant?" He remembered the first time he'd talked to Brianna, but he wasn't sure if they'd met in a store or something and he'd forgotten.

"Yes, silly. The first time I waited on you, it was in the summer. You asked for a strawberry salad and an Arnold Palmer. Later, you even asked for a slice of strawberry pie. I thought it was adorable."

"I really like strawberries." *Shut up, Nate.*

"I waited over a year for you to notice me. The day you came to Yoder's and asked me to come outside to see you?"

"Yes?"

"That was a pretty big day in my life." She smiled. "I don't regret saying yes, Nate." She lowered her voice. "And even though I probably shouldn't admit such a thing, I also don't regret kissing you."

"No?" His voice squeaked.

"Not at all. You see, no matter how you might think of me, I know how I feel about you. I love you, Nate. And, no, I don't expect you to love me back yet." While he stared at her, she chuckled softly. "Now, you can say what you've wanted to say."

Brianna loved him. She didn't want to slap his face or never see him again. "I had a lot of things to tell you, but I'm pretty sure none of it matters except for one thing."

"Which is?"

He reached for both of her hands. "I love you too."

They looked at each other and smiled.

"This might be a good time to kiss me again, Nate Beachy."

"You think so?"

"I do. Especially since we're alone, it's dark, and we're not even standing on a street corner."

Nate reckoned he was likely not worthy of Brianna. She was lovely, made better choices, and was far more eloquent than he could ever hope to be. But at least he wasn't a fool.

Gently pressing both of his hands to her cheeks, he brushed his lips against hers. Then kissed her softly. When he felt her tremble, he held her close. "I love you, Brianna. Thank you for waiting for me."

"You were worth it."

He couldn't help but smile. That was everything he ever needed to know.

29

August was pretty sure that he'd never had a worse day at the golf course. From the time he'd started working at six, one problem after another surfaced. Two of the sprinkler heads died, someone ignored the signs to stay off a freshly patched section of turf and ruined it, the humidity had turned up about nine notches, and a foursome of college boys had tried to play without paying — and then had argued about it.

His aunt and uncle had been gone all morning to a funeral. Avery, one of his recent teen hires, had called in sick. Finally, topping it all off, they'd run out of dollar bills, which most of his Amish golfers had taken as a personal affront. August had not only been forced to listen to at least five lectures about good practices, but one cranky old guy had shaken his finger at him.

It had been one of those days where practically everything that could go wrong had gone wrong. Because of that, August had never been happier to turn the "open" sign to "closed" and go to his apartment.

It was dark when he got there. Though he usually lit the battery-operated light, he bypassed it and went directly to the shower. After enjoying a blast of cold, he turned the water to as hot as he could stand it and then stood under the rejuvenating spray for several minutes. Only when the knots around his neck and shoulders loosened did he get out.

By the time he got dressed and went to his small kitchenette and living room, August was in a far better mood.

And then he saw the hastily written note.

August, Gideon and I had to go to a meeting that we couldn't get out of, but I wanted to let you know that your mother called. She said your father is doing better, praise God. I'm also sorry to say that she let me know that they're still wondering when you are flying in. You are supposed to email them with your flight information. For some reason, she thought Gideon and I were buying your plane ticket? That's not right, is it?

"No, it is not," he said out loud. Gritting

his teeth, he continued to read.

Anyway, I'm sorry to leave all this in a long note, but I wanted you to know what's going on before you head over to see Betsy. We love you, August. Try not to fret.

He didn't want to fret. He really didn't. But how could he not? Instead of emailing him back or arranging another Skype, his mother had called and left that message with his aunt. It wasn't right for his mother to tell Diane things that she knew weren't true.

Lifting the note, August read it again. He looked up at the ceiling and said out loud, "God, please be with me. I think I'm going to need You now more than ever."

Determined to take care of things once and for all, he went downstairs and logged in to the computer. August would've tried to Skype, but with the time difference, it wasn't possible at the moment. He decided to write his parents a note.

This one was short, to the point, and as civil as he was able to be.

Dear Mamm and Daed, I am grateful that Daed is better. Daed, with the Lord's help, I hope you will continue to heal.

292

I am not coming to Namibia. As much as I want to be the son you need, I am not a missionary. I can't pretend to be anything other than what I am.

I know you don't understand, and I don't expect you to. I love you both.

August

He pressed send and paused. Sure that he would feel regret or remorse, August stood and stared at the blank screen and waited for the guilt that was sure to come. However, all he felt was relief. As hard as it was not to do as his parents asked, he knew he had no choice. It was time all three of them learned that he was his own man.

Glad that the task was done, he went back to his apartment, made himself a quick sandwich, and then finally headed over to the one place he wanted to be — with Betsy.

Betsy was now staying with her parents. They'd rented a house near Pinecraft Park. When he arrived, he noticed that it was one of the newer homes there. The owners had built a wide front porch and planted a profusion of trees and shrubs. All of it was white, even the front porch and the wicker chairs at rest on it.

He smiled when he saw Betsy sitting in a pink dress on one of the chairs. She was reading a book and had a glass of water next to her. He had never seen a prettier sight in his life.

She didn't look up until he was halfway up the front walk. But then a beautiful smile appeared on her face. "You're here."

He chuckled. "I am at that." When she moved to stand up, he motioned for her to sit down. "No need for that. I'll sit right here beside you."

She nibbled her bottom lip. "I should get you something to drink too. Would you care for lemonade?"

August didn't think he'd be able to think about sipping lemonade on a girl's front porch without smiling ever again. "I'm gut. Don't worry about me." He studied her face. Noticed some dark circles under her eyes. "How are you feeling?"

"Much better, I'm happy to say."

"I'm happy to hear it. If you're certain . . ."

She crossed her legs. "Why am I getting the feeling that you aren't so sure that I am?"

"No reason . . . other than you have some new shadows under your eyes." Feeling bad for even mentioning them, he added quickly, "Forget I said anything, okay? I think you look lovely."

Some of the joy evaporated from her expression. "Well, actually, I haven't been sleeping all that well." She glanced toward the glass storm door, obviously looking for her parents. "I'm on steroids, which helps my lungs but wreaks havoc with my sleeping. I'm on such a strong dose that the medicine makes me antsy."

That sounded terrible. "Betsy, can't they give you something for that?"

"They can, but then I'd be on yet another set of pills, which brings on another set of problems." She shrugged. "It's all okay, August. I'm used to the side effects."

"Are you still going to stay here a little longer or do your parents want you to go home right away?"

"I'm staying." She smiled softly. "Actually, I'm going to stay here even longer than anticipated."

"Betsy, really?"

Her smile widened. "Guess what? I might even be here permanently. Sarasota is on a list of one of the best places in the country to live if one has asthma. What a blessing is that?"

"It's an amazing blessing." It also sounded too good to be true. Could the Lord really be so good to them? "Are you sure about Sarasota being on that list?"

It was obvious his reaction wasn't quite what she'd hoped it would be. "Boy, you are sure a doubting Thomas today."

"I'm sorry. I guess I'm afraid to hope."

Her gaze warmed. "The hospital administrator gave my parents a booklet about the hospital and the city. You should've seen their faces when the report discussed how this city's facilities, combined with the warmer climate in the winter, help people like me."

"Wow. I'm sorry, but I bet your parents weren't too happy about that."

"Oh, they weren't! Not at all. Not even a little bit. But then, once they got over the shock, they started seeing the benefits of me finally growing up and being on my own."

"I'm so glad that Sarasota is a good place for your health. Having you here is going to be terrific."

"I think so . . . especially since you're here." Before he could say a word about that, she slapped a hand over her mouth. "August, please forgive me. Will you be here? Or are you still thinking about going to Africa to help your parents at the mission?"

"There's nothing to forgive. I want you to be here. I'd love it. And . . . I decided not to go to Africa."

"I'm glad, but I have a feeling that news isn't going to be real well received, either."

"It won't. Something happened, so I ended up writing them a note this afternoon. I'm sure when we Skype again, I'll hear how disappointed they are in me."

"I'm so sorry."

"I am too." Looking at her intently, he added, "Betsy, I realized that I need to follow my own path. It wasn't right for either my parents or me to think that I would be the best person to serve there. They deserve someone who is not only trained and experienced but who wants to be there."

"Someone who is following his heart, not merely there because of duty."

"Exactly." He exhaled. "No matter how much I tried to feel compelled to go, I just didn't. I love my parents, but I want to follow my own path."

She smiled. "You have your own life list."

"I guess I do. The path I'm on might not be the best one or the path that inspires other people. But I am certain that it's the best one for me."

"The Lord did give you Gideon and Diane," Betsy pointed out. "He gave you an aunt and uncle who had a business that you enjoy. There's nothing wrong with that.

Honestly, I think there's everything right about it."

"I hope so."

"I know so."

The storm door opened and both Mr. and Mrs. Detweiler came out. Mr. Detweiler had a bowl of pretzels and Mrs. Detweiler was holding a tray of drinks. August stood up to help Betsy's mother put the tray down.

"We won't stay too long," Mr. Detweiler said. "We did want to say hello, though."

"I'm glad to see you again — under better circumstances," August said politely. Looking at Betsy, he added, "I'm so glad Betsy's feeling better."

Mrs. Detweiler smiled at her daughter. "That is the greatest blessing. Our prayers have been answered, for sure and for certain."

"We're also blessed to be able to rent this place for a whole week. Going back and forth to the hospital is always tough."

"I imagine so." He folded his hands behind his back, not sure what to say next.

Betsy piped up. "Mamm, Daed, August decided to stay here. He's not going to Africa."

August wished she wouldn't have blurted that to her parents, but he supposed they'd find out sooner or later. "I only just made the decision. I wrote my parents just a little while ago."

Neither Mr. nor Mrs. Detweiler looked appalled. Actually, Betsy's parents looked like they understood.

"What did they say?" Mrs. Detweiler asked.

"I don't know. My mother is busy, so sometimes it takes her a while to answer emails. I'm sure she'll be disappointed, though."

Mrs. Detweiler glanced at her daughter. "I don't know if this will help, but I've recently learned that when we raise our children to grow up, we have to allow them to do just that. Even if their wishes and choices don't exactly mesh with ours."

"I hope my parents will be as gracious about that realization as you two are."

"They will," Mr. Detweiler said. "It might take time for them to come around to your point of view, but they will."

"I hope you're right."

Mrs. Detweiler edged toward the door. "Well, we just wanted to say hello. I think we'll take our drinks and go back inside."

Mr. Detweiler grinned. "Jah. Fawn and me were so inspired by Betsy's list, we're working on a life list of our own."

"It's catching on like wildfire," August

said. "Do you have anything on your list yet?"

Mrs. Detweiler nodded. "Believe it or not, I never learned how to ride a horse properly. I can hitch one to a buggy, drive it, brush and feed it, and even do a decent job of cleaning its hooves. But I've always been scared to sit on a horse's back with a saddle. I'm going to give it a try."

"You too, Mr. Detweiler?"

"Nee. I've always wanted to read more history books. I'm going to start learning more about Lewis and Clark."

"I canna help you with that."

"No need. That's what the library is for, ain't so?" Mr. Detweiler joked as they went back inside.

When they were alone again, August said, "Betsy, I'm happy for you. I'm glad you feel better and that your parents are once again your biggest supporters."

"Danke." She smiled at him, and then glanced away. "I guess all we have to do now is figure out when we can have that golf game."

"You still want to play a round of golf?"

"Of course I do! I want to pull my cart and get through all eighteen holes."

"Eighteen is a lot," he warned. "It's going to take hours."

"August, I didn't begin my life list just to quit. I'm going to play that round of golf, no matter what. Of course, the question might be . . . will you still play golf with me?"

"Of course." His heart was so full, he smiled at her. "Don't even think about playing with anyone else."

30

A couple of hours after August left, Mary came over. Betsy was so happy. She needed to reconnect with her and get some advice. She really needed some advice.

They went to Betsy's bedroom. It was a clean, small bedroom with only a double bed, a wooden bedside table, and an assortment of pegs and hooks on the wall. The walls were white, and the wooden floors had no rug. All in all, it was very stark. As far as Betsy was concerned, the only warm and pretty feature in the room was an around the world quilt in shades of yellow and purple.

Mary looked around the room. "It sure is clean in here."

Though it was a pretty mediocre compliment, the truth couldn't be denied. "It *is* very clean. Though the quilt is lovely, I find it jarring to be in here. It's far too plain."

Mary sniffed as she sat down on the edge

of the bed. "Sorry, but it also smells of Pine-Sol."

"Oh, I know. At least it has its own bathroom. I'm glad I don't have to share one with my parents."

"It's better than the hospital, as well," Mary added, obviously trying to think of positive things to say about the drab little space.

"It is at that. It's not as pretty as your home, though."

"I wish you were still there."

Betsy did too, but she'd also gotten a better understanding of her parents' perspective during the last two days. Or maybe she was the one who had gotten a reality check. She couldn't deny that her asthma attack had scared her. If Mary and Jayson hadn't heard her in the middle of the night — and called for an ambulance — Betsy knew that she might not have survived.

It was time to stop acting as if her asthma was just a minor inconvenience and learn to take it more seriously.

"I'm so glad I was at your house when I had my attack," she said. "You and Jayson saved my life. Thank you for everything you did."

"You're welcome. Now, tell me what your plans are."

After briefly filling her in about the latest developments, including the strong chance that she might actually come back to Sarasota to live, Betsy said, "Can we talk about something else now?"

"Of course. We can talk about whatever you want."

"All right, here goes." She took a fortifying breath. "How did you know Jayson was the one?"

Mary's eyes lit up. She reached for Betsy's hand. "Betsy! Are you wondering if August is the man for you?"

"Oh, I'm not wondering, Mary. I really do think he is. But I'm doubting myself too."

"Why? He's wonderful. And it's obvious he cares for you."

She wrinkled her nose. "Maybe I simply have Pinecraft fever or something."

Mary blinked. "What in the world is that?"

"It's the fact that everything here in Pinecraft seems better. The weather is prettier, the flowers brighter . . ." She smiled. "Even the pie seems to taste better here."

Mary burst out laughing. "Are you trying to tell me that you suspect August is part of your Pinecraft fever? Like, he might not be as wonderful-gut if you stuck him in the middle of Kentucky?"

Betsy squirmed in embarrassment. "Okay,

I guess it's a silly comparison. But to an extent . . . jah. I like him so much, but maybe it's just because I'm on vacation and he's so handsome and kind?"

"Hmm. I can see your point."

"So . . . was there a moment when you knew Jayson was the man for you?"

"Jah." Mary frowned. "It probably wasn't the moment you are hoping to hear about, though."

"I'm really looking for some good advice and insight. Please, just tell me."

"Okay, I knew Jayson was the one when he told me that he was almost promised to another woman and he'd kept it a secret."

"But that was an awful moment!" Mary had come back to the Marigold Inn and cried for hours.

"Jah, it was. No doubt about it, I was devastated. I was sure my heart was broken."

"I'm surprised that's when you knew you were in love." Actually, she'd been hoping for a rainbows-and-unicorns type of moment, not one filled with tears and turmoil.

Mary's voice lowered. "I knew I liked Jayson a lot before he told me about the other woman. I was even pretty sure I was falling in love with him. But I didn't realize that I'd *already* fallen in love until I thought that he was out of my life forever." She shifted on the bed. "Weeks later, when Jayson came to Trail and called on me with his sister, I knew I wanted to be his wife for the rest of my life."

Betsy was struggling to keep up. "You knew because he apologized?"

She shook her head. "Nee. I knew because I'd seen just how hard a relationship with him might be — yet I still wanted to be by his side."

"You wanted him through good times and bad."

"Exactly." She smiled at last. "It took me a moment, but that's what I realized at long last. That a great relationship with Jayson wasn't about walks on the beach at Siesta Key or flirting with him or even realizing how much we had in common. It had to do with trust and respect and compassion and grace. And love, of course."

Trust. Respect. Compassion. Grace. Love. "It had nothing to do with Pinecraft fever."

Mary nodded. "I can honestly say that being married to Jayson and living here in Pinecraft is wonderful. Jayson makes me feel happy and treasured. Together, we've even made several couple friends, so I'm far from being the wallflower I once was. The weather is also nice, and I still love walking on the beach. But all of that doesn't matter when I see Jayson across the room and I know that he's mine."

"Wow."

"Uh-oh. Did I give you too much to think about?"

"No. You made me realize that August and I could have everything you and Jayson do."

"But?"

"But there's time to be sure."

Mary smiled. "I promise, Betsy, that one day you'll know that either August isn't the man for you . . . or that he's your one and only. There won't be a doubt in your mind — and you'll realize that you're willing to do everything you can possibly do to be with him."

"I'll let you know when that happens."

She winked. "Just be prepared. That moment might come along sooner than you think."

31

Annie felt like crying. Betsy was about to come over for her very last swimming lesson. Though Danielle had tried to extend her visit, the landlord had held firm. She had another set of guests arriving right after Independence Day. She and Danielle needed to be out by the agreed-upon date.

Betsy had come over two days previously, armed with pamphlets that she'd received from her doctor's office. They'd recommended that she try to swim at least twice a week. The exercise was good for her lungs. With a smile, she'd even shared that her parents had helped her research recreation centers so that if she did move to Pinecraft, she could easily follow the doctor's orders.

Danielle had been a nervous wreck when Betsy had first stepped into the pool. At first, she'd even tried to persuade Betsy to stay in the shallow end, "just in case" something happened. But to everyone's surprise, it had been Betsy who'd been adamant about swimming in the deep end. "I want to be a swimmer, Danny," she said in her sweet, slightly Kentucky-accented voice. "You made me believe I could do this."

And so Danielle had taken Betsy out to the deep end. And, with Annie hovering, she encouraged Betsy to swim. And she had.

Now, after their final lesson, they were going to have a party of sorts. Of course she and Danielle had gone a little overboard. They'd bought decorations, a gift, and a strawberry pie from Yoder's.

When Annie went inside, she spied her sister sitting in the living room. The lights were off and it was completely quiet.

"Hey, are you all right?"

Danielle glanced up at her. "Yeah. Just a little melancholy, I suppose. I don't want this trip to end."

Annie perched on the couch next to her. "I don't either. Danny, in case I haven't told you enough, I'm really glad you asked me to stay with you this month. Thank you."

She winked. "You're probably just saying that because you met Jack. Handsome, rich, perfectly perfect Jack."

Annie chuckled. "He is all those things, but that's not what I meant."

309

"I know." Her expression turned more thoughtful. "Annie, to be honest, I wasn't sure how the two of us would do together for four weeks. It felt like an eternity. When I asked you, I was just so sick of trying to pretend that I was fine. And so tired of everyone always acting as if Peter had been right to divorce me."

She paused. "Annie, I was afraid to be alone and you were the only person I knew who might not say no to me."

Annie's heart ached for her. "Everyone is going to come around. All you have to do is be more open with them."

"Do you think that will help smooth things over with my kids?"

"I think it's a good start."

"I should've been more honest with them and I shouldn't have kept so much inside. I treated everyone around me so badly. I've got a lot of work to do to make amends."

"One step at a time, right?"

"I just hope they realize that I really do love them so much."

"They will, Danielle. Maybe things won't get better next week, but they will eventually. I promise, they love you too."

Reaching for her hand, she said, "Annie, I'm really glad you came. Thanks for taking a chance, even if you weren't sure if you wanted to take it."

Annie clasped her other hand over their linked fingers. "We need to stop talking before we both burst into tears."

"I agree." When the doorbell rang, Danny's eyes lit up. "Here's our girl."

Together, they hurried to the door.

Betsy was standing on the other side holding both a pie and two gift bags as well as her backpack.

"Here, let me help you," Annie said as she took the pie out of her hands. "Did you carry all of this on the bus? I wish you would've let one of us pick you up."

"I got an Uber. I figured it was a special occasion. And don't worry. One of you can drive me home."

"Come in, dear. And prepare yourself. We've been decorating."

When they went out to the pool, Betsy giggled. "Is all of this just for the three of us or did you invite half the population of Longboat Key?"

"It's for just us three." Danielle looked a little sheepish. "I guess we couldn't help ourselves."

Betsy put her gift bags on the table next to the one Annie and Danny had set out. "To be honest, I was kind of hoping you two would do something like this. It

311

wouldn't feel the same if you didn't."

After putting Betsy's coconut cream pie in the refrigerator, Danielle said, "What do you think? Are you ready to swim?"

"I am. I even have a new bathing suit for the occasion." She carefully unpinned her dress and showed off her modest royal blue bathing suit. "What do you think?"

"You look great," Annie said.

Betsy looked down at her legs. "I told my mother that I think I'm getting more toned, thanks to all the walking, golfing, and swimming I've been doing."

"The shadows under your eyes have faded too," Danielle added. "That's a blessing."

"I've been taking better care of myself. I'm determined to keep doing that too."

"Are you ready to swim?"

"I am. Which stroke first?"

Danielle nodded. "I thought maybe we should do your least favorite part of swimming first."

"That means I have to go under water, right?"

"I'm afraid so," Danny said. "But you've been doing really well."

"I'm going to be nearby too," Annie reminded her. "And we're not trying to make you hold your breath for any length of time. All you have to do is swim a little bit under water and then pop back up."

Betsy's face was determined. "I'm ready."

In they went. To Betsy's credit, she immediately ducked her head under water and popped up easily. When she and Danielle started swimming across the width of the pool, bobbing up for breaths, Annie felt like a proud mother hen. Betsy had come so far.

And so they continued. Freestyle came next, followed by the backstroke and then breaststroke. As Annie had hoped, each stroke was a little bit more solid and stronger than the last. Betsy did the breaststroke the entire length of the pool.

When she got to the end, Danielle hugged her tight. "You did great! I'm going to remember this day for the rest of my life, Betsy."

"Me too. But Danielle, you're coming back, right?"

"Well, I hope so . . ."

"No, I mean, we're friends now," Betsy pressed. "I want to see you even if we're not anywhere near the pool."

And that's when Danielle almost burst into tears. Annie could see her trying her best to hold it together. She turned away and breathed deeply.

"Okay, Betsy. Let's swim back to the shallow end and then eat pie and open presents."

"What stroke?"

"Any one you want. Annie, come on. You too."

The three of them kicked off from the side and slowly swam back to the steps on the shallow end, Betsy in between them. When they got out, Danielle put on music and got out the pies.

Annie sliced pie and Betsy arranged the pieces on plates. They tapped forks before they dug in.

"Here's to life lists and ladies who make them happen," Betsy said.

"Here's to young women named Betsy who make other people believe in life lists too," Annie added.

After taking a couple of more bites, Danielle said, "Annie, don't let me refuse a slice of Yoder's pie ever again. This is so good."

"Don't worry, I won't, especially when we put two slices on the same plate."

Betsy shook her head. "You two ladies are so funny. You always enjoy food so much yet talk about how you shouldn't eat it."

"It's from a lifetime of restraint, I guess," Danielle said. "I'm starting to think I should have eaten more pie and complained less."

"There's something for your life list,

then." Betsy jabbed a strawberry with her fork.

"I have a feeling you're right." Gesturing toward everyone's near-empty plates, Danielle said, "Who's ready to open presents?"

"All of us, of course," Annie teased. She picked up Betsy's gift bag and handed it to her, then retrieved the gift bags Betsy had brought for them. "Who first?"

"Betsy," Danielle said.

"Okay." Pushing her plate to one side, she placed the bag on her lap and pulled out some tissue paper, then the first item. It was a puzzle highlighting about a dozen national parks. "Thank you," she said, but it was obvious that she was confused by the gift.

"The puzzle was my idea," Annie said. "You see, I've been thinking about your life list. Even though visiting these places might be more in the 'bucket list' category, I thought it might be fun for you to think about visiting some of them one day. I even looked it up. The Amish have bus trips to all sorts of places."

Her eyes brightened. "I like that idea. Thank you."

"Go on now. There's more." Danielle pointed to the bag.

Betsy dug in again and pulled out a pair of swim goggles and a rubber swim cap.

"Oh! I'm going to look just like a real swim-mer!"

"That's because you are. Now you can swim all you want without getting your hair wet. And . . . you'll be able to see things when you put your face in the water."

"I love them, Danielle."

"There's one last thing, Betsy," Annie said.

"You two shouldn't have spent so much money." She dug in and pulled out an envelope. She opened and read their silly card, which had cats and a rather cheesy poem about friendship. But then her eyes widened when she spied the gift certificate to The Boardwalk, the restaurant where An-nie and Jack had eaten. "This is a really nice restaurant. What's this for?"

"Have you heard of it?"

"Jah. My friend Esther's husband Michael works there."

"Really? Betsy, I know Michael! He's my favorite waiter."

"He's a nice man. He's going to be pleased to see me there. But you shouldn't have spent so much."

"Did the amount ring a bell?" Danielle asked. "Because sixty dollars is how much you gave us for the lessons. We put it to one side and used it for the gift certificate."

"Now you can take your girlfriends, or

maybe your August, out to dinner there," Annie said.

"I'll love that." She carefully put the gift certificate back in the envelope with the card. "Now it's time for the two of you to open your gifts."

Annie noticed that Betsy's eyes were shining. She was as excited to give them their presents as they'd been to give Betsy hers. It really was better to give than receive. "Should we open them at the same time, or should one of us go first?"

"You can open them at the same time. I got you both the same present."

Exchanging a smile with Danielle, Annie pulled out her own batch of tissue paper, then lifted up a small wooden sign, the kind that was designed to sit on a counter or a bookshelf. It said "A Sister Is God Giving One an Instant Best Friend."

A lump formed in her throat. "Oh my."

"As soon as I saw that sign in a shop, I knew I would get you each one. I have an older brother who I love very much. But you two make me wish I had a sister. I love how close you are. You two are so different, but you seem to value each other's differences. You both are blessed."

Danielle wasn't even trying to hold back tears. "Betsy, thank you. This . . . well, this means more to me than you'll ever know."

"I feel the same way," Annie said. "It's a really wonderful gift."

Half an hour later, Betsy hugged Danielle goodbye then got in the car with Annie. As Annie drove down the two-lane road to the edge of Longboat Key, crossed over the bridge, and then entered Sarasota proper, neither of them said much. Annie was grateful for that. Even though she doubted she'd be saying goodbye for very long — she and Danielle had already discussed renting a house in February or March — this moment felt bittersweet. The next time they met, it would be a reunion. This visit, with all the awkwardness and hardship and excitement and joy? Well, it had been special.

"It's this street," Betsy said. "And that white house with the white wicker chairs on the porch."

When Annie parked in front of the house, she said, "Danielle and I put our phone numbers in the card. Our home addresses are there too."

"I know. I'll call and write." Smiling, she added, "I put my parents' phone number and address in my card too."

"Please take care of yourself, okay? Keep swimming and follow your doctor's orders."

318

"Annie, not you too? Everyone is telling me to do that."

"That's because everyone loves you, Betsy." She playfully wagged a finger. "You're not allowed to scare us like that ever again."

"I'll do my best not to." She reached out and hugged Annie. "Danke, Annie. Thank you for everything."

"You are very welcome. See you soon."

Betsy smiled at her before picking up her bag and getting out of the car.

Annie watched her walk up the steps, pause at the door, and turn back to her. When she waved goodbye, Annie raised her hand to do the same.

And then, Betsy was gone.

Driving back to Danielle's house, Annie gave thanks. Thanks for just about every-thing.

32

Betsy and her mother had rented bicycles, and for the first time ever, they rode together. By the time they arrived at the Snow Bird Golf Course, her mother was shaking her head in disbelief. "This was so fun. I can't believe I always said no to doing things like this with you."

Betsy was tired of regrets. "At least we're doing it now."

"That is true," her mother said as she hopped off her bike. "And look at that. Your father is already here."

"I had no doubt that he would be." They'd already made arrangements for her father to meet them there so he could ride her bike back to the bike shop. August had warned them that Betsy was going to be tired after playing eighteen holes of golf. He'd arranged for a driver to take them both to lunch near her rental house.

Taking her purse out of the bike's basket,

Betsy smiled at the three men standing on the patio in front of the pro shop. August, his uncle Gideon, and her father were all watching her and her mother approach.

"Do you think they look surprised or just really pleased?" Mamm whispered.

"I'm going to choose pleased."

She grinned. "Me too." Speaking more loudly, she said, "We had a great bike ride, but I need a cup of water."

"I have some bottles already on ice for you," Gideon said. "Come on in."

After drinking half a bottle of water and freshening up, Betsy smiled at August. "I'm ready when you are."

"Let's go, then. Grab a score card and a pencil, Bets."

"Wait, we're going to keep score?"

"Absolutely. We're going to do this right. Where's your glove?"

"I have it." She pretended to act a little annoyed at his ordering her about, but they both knew she didn't care that he was telling her what to do. It was just a golf game, but it was a big deal to her. She was excited and nervous. Not about getting too tired or hot but about getting so frustrated with herself that she'd want to stop after the first four or five holes. She wanted to be able to say that she played an entire round of golf at least once in her life. For better or worse, today was the day.

"Have a good time, you two," Gideon said. "August, don't forget that the boys are coming in early. The three of us will handle things from here."

"Danke, Uncle."

"Just to make sure I understand, the round will take several hours and then you're going to lunch?" her mother asked.

August nodded. "I reckon we'll be playing for four hours at the very least."

"Lunch will be another two hours, Mamm," Betsy said. "I'll be home late this afternoon. Maybe even this evening."

"We're going to Siesta Key for the day. Have a good time. I have my cell phone," Daed said.

"If something happens, I'll call," August promised.

Finally, at long last, she and August were guiding their push carts to the first hole.

"Don't forget, we're going to the women's tees." He pointed to the blue markers.

"I haven't forgotten."

"Get out your driver. Or would you rather use your 9 iron?"

"I'll try my driver first."

Looking like a doting father, he handed her a tee and a golf ball. "Remember how to set up your shot?"

"I think so, but feel free to advise."

He knelt on the green. "Right about here, I think."

Carefully, she pressed in the golf tee and arranged the ball on top of it. Holding the driver, she said, "I guess this is it."

"Take a couple of practice swings. Easy now," he cautioned as she swung the club a few times.

It was now or never, especially since she had to do this seventeen more times. "I'm ready. Any last piece of advice?"

"Jah." He walked to her side and kissed her cheek. "If all else fails, remember this is a game. It's actually supposed to be fun."

She was so surprised by both his words and his kiss, she burst out laughing. Then walked right up to the tee, arranged the club, her head, her stance, and her feet. Took a deep breath and swung.

The ball went two feet.

She glanced back at August. The moment he met her eyes, his worried frown vanished. "Okay. It's time to take another shot."

"What about you?"

"Me, well, I, uh, thought maybe I'd forgo playing every hole."

She shook her head. "Even I know how this game works, August Troyer. Go to your tee box and tee off." Betsy stood to the side as August walked to the men's tee, pulled out his driver, quickly put down his golf tee and ball, and then swung the club. It sailed through the sky. She could kind-of-sort-of see it land near the flag on the putting green. "Gut job," she said.

"I've probably played this course a hundred times, Betsy."

"I understand. I'm not comparing us." Well, not too much. "This is fun," she reminded herself as she reached for her trusty 9 iron and walked down the course.

And so it continued.

By the time Betsy teed off at the fifth hole, her ball usually went about four or five feet. It was still a slog, though. No matter whether the hole was a par three or four or five, it seemed to take her ten to twelve hits to get the ball into the hole.

When they reached the ninth hole, August insisted they sit down and take a water break. Two groups played through. They'd been playing over four hours. She was sweaty, her arms and back were sore, and she was pretty sure that her nose was sunburned. August didn't look that much better.

"Are you all right?"

"I'm good."

"Nine holes is a good first start . . ."

"It's not eighteen. I'm doing it. I'm having fun."

He grinned. "Me too."

Four holes later, August handed her another water bottle. "Betsy, you've played thirteen holes. I know plenty of men who don't last that long on their first round of golf. Would you like to stop?"

"Nee."

"Are you sure?"

"Yes. I'm going to do this. I'm going to play eighteen holes."

"I don't want you to get too tired."

"August Troyer, my lungs are fine. Stop worrying. I'm having fun." Okay, she absolutely was not having fun, but she was feeling determined and proud.

He sighed. "Off you go, then."

It took her twelve strokes to get through the fourteenth hole, thirteen to get through fifteen, eleven for sixteen and a whopping seventeen strokes at the seventeenth hole, thanks to a sand trap.

When they finally, finally reached the eighteenth tee box, Betsy felt as proud of herself as if she'd climbed a giant mountain. After August teed off and his ball went sailing, she positioned her ball at the tee box for the very last time that day.

"Thank You, God," she whispered as she took a warm-up swing. "Thank You for being with me and helping me every step of the way."

Realizing that she no longer cared about the number of strokes or making a good impression, Betsy eyed the white ball, exhaled, and hit. And that ball went flying.

"August," she whispered. Turning on her heel, she faced him. "August! Did you see that?"

He was grinning ear to ear. "I sure did. It was a beautiful drive, Betsy. Gorgeous."

She shoved her club in the bag. "Come on, we need to see where it went!"

Side by side, they walked down the fairway. When they were at the halfway mark, she spied her ball. "That's me, isn't it?"

He nodded. "See where you're going?" He pointed to the flag. "Hit it nice and easy now."

When the ball popped up in the air and then plopped on the ground just a few feet away, August looked at her warily. "Okay?"

Betsy couldn't resist laughing. "Of course. I'm no Tiger Woods yet, am I?"

"On a positive note, at least you know who he is now."

Fifteen minutes later, when she putted her ball into the eighteenth hole, Betsy dropped her putter on the ground and hurried over to him. August was ready. He picked her up and twirled her around — just like he had their first time at the putting green.

Betsy couldn't help it, tears were in her eyes. Even learning to put her face in the water hadn't felt as daunting as this round of golf. But she'd done it.

"I'm so proud of you, Betsy." He set her back on the ground but didn't release his hands from around her waist. "I don't think I've ever met another person who is as stubborn as you are."

As compliments went, she reckoned it probably wasn't all that good. But to her? Well, it was a good one, because she knew it to be true. She was stubborn. "Thank you?"

He laughed. "How about this? I am proud of you, Betsy. I'm proud of you and I love you something fierce."

Yes. That was much better. "I love you something fierce right back, August."

He held out his hand. "Let's put everything away and get out of here."

She took his hand and walked by his side. She was exhausted, hot, and sweaty. But she was also loved by August Troyer.

"Did you play all eighteen, girly?" an old man called out as they approached the pro shop.

"I sure did!"

"Did you now?" He whistled low. "That ain't easy."

"You're right, it wasn't."

The older man lifted up his sunglasses. "Well, what did you think? Did you have a good time?"

She couldn't resist smiling from ear to ear. "I sure did. As a matter of fact, I had a great time!"

"That's all that matters, ain't so?"

"Jah." When they walked inside the shop and the door closed behind them, Betsy was no longer able to contain her mirth. She burst out laughing. When August joined her, Betsy decided that she couldn't have asked for a better moment.

33

The three of them were crammed next to each other in front of the computer monitor. Uncle Gideon was perched on a stool, August was in the desk's wooden chair, and Aunt Diane had elected to stand. As the computer struggled to make the Skype connection, Gideon frowned as he looked around the small space.

"One day we should make things a little nicer in here," he said.

"How do you think we should do that?" Diane asked in a dry tone. "Do you want to put golf pictures up on the walls?"

"How about we start with a bigger desk with room for two chairs instead of just one?"

As the computer beeped and appeared to almost connect but then didn't, Diane sighed. "It's all gonna be up to August anyway. We're going to be sleeping in and relaxing."

"And maybe I'll finally get myself a pool, now that I'll have time to enjoy it."

August hid a smile. Though his aunt and uncle had always talked about retiring, they'd finally decided to do so just the night before. Betsy's bout in the hospital — along with her life list — had encouraged them to stop waiting. When August had come downstairs from his apartment that morning, both Gideon and Diane had been waiting for him. By the time he'd finished his first cup of coffee, Gideon had announced that not only were they handing over the golf course to him, but they were going to give him their small house, which was directly behind the pro shop.

It turned out that they'd saved a lot of money over the years, plus Diane's parents had bequeathed her quite a bit when they'd died. Diane and Gideon planned to get a small house farther inland and spend their mornings gardening and evenings sitting on their front porch instead of being constantly surrounded by people.

It was a lot for August to take in, especially since they'd also decided to join him for the morning's Skype visit with his parents. August knew his mamm and daed wouldn't be happy about Diane and Gideon being there, but his aunt and uncle didn't care.

They wanted to give August support.

"Finally!" Gideon exclaimed as the beeping and buzzing stopped and the connection finalized.

August took a deep breath.

"Don't forget that all four of us love you," Diane whispered. "It'll be all right."

He was gazing up at her when his parents appeared on the screen. His father looked ragged. Easily twenty pounds lighter than three weeks ago. His mother looked tired, but there was an anger simmering in her eyes as she stared at Gideon and Diane.

"What are they doing here?" she asked.

"Hello to you too, Charity," Diane said. Her voice softened. "Hello, David. I'm glad you're doing better."

He nodded. "Danke. The Lord worked a small miracle, I think. For a while there I feared that I'd be seeing our parents far sooner than I'd imagined."

"God is good," Gideon said.

"He is always good," August's mother pronounced, as if Gideon had been attempting to say otherwise.

August shifted uneasily, trying to take Diane's words to heart. So far neither of his parents had said a word to him. He hoped it wasn't intentional — and that they were merely stunned by Gideon's and Diane's presence. He wasn't sure, though.

"Hi, Mamm and Daed. Daed, I'm really glad you're better."

"It's good I am, isn't it? Otherwise I don't know what would've happened to your mother."

August wasn't sure what to say. That he knew his mother would be grieving if Daed had died? "Yes, well . . ."

His mother's expression was as harsh as her tone of voice. "I know what would've happened. I would've had to say goodbye to everyone here because we couldn't continue our work."

It took a second to realize that, once again, they were only fixated on the mission, not on anything else. He swallowed.

"Charity, you know that was uncalled for," Gideon chided. "You shouldn't have expected the boy to have left his whole life for ya. It wasn't right."

"Our lives are none of your business, Gideon. You shouldn't have joined August. This is a private conversation."

"I'm surprised to hear you say that," Diane said. "So far, you've barely spoken to the boy." She glowered. "Except to tell him that you're disappointed in him."

His father inhaled sharply. "Diane, you are out of line."

Her chin lifted. "If I am, then I'm in good company."

It was time to intervene. "Stop, everyone. Mamm, Daed, I did want to talk to you about a lot of things, but not about me not going to Africa. That's already been covered."

"What do you have to say?" Mamm asked.

"I want you to know that I met someone. I've fallen in love. Her name is Betsy and she's wonderful."

"Where did you meet her?" Daed asked.

He couldn't help but smile at the memory. "Here on the golf course. She was walking down the fairway. I had to shoo her out of the way so she wouldn't get hit by a ball."

"She's a golfer?" His father didn't sound happy at all.

"Not really. Betsy just wanted to learn. You see, she's got this life —"

"Is she even Amish?" Mamm asked.

"She is. She's New Order, just like we are."

"She's a lovely, sweet girl," Uncle Gideon added. "She will be a gut partner for August."

"So you two met her?" his mother asked, obviously speaking to Gideon and Diane.

"Of course we have," Diane said. "Actually, poor Betsy was in the hospital the same time as you were, David." She placed a hand on August's shoulder. "This young man had a lot on his plate for a few days. No doubt about that."

"It was nothing to how I was feeling," his mother said.

"You've really disappointed me, August," Daed added.

He could practically feel both his aunt and uncle bristle. Ironically, though, August suddenly felt at peace. It was like he'd needed witnesses to see exactly how self-centered his parents could be. It was time to stop hoping they would treat him differently. "I love you both and wish you well. Daed, I hope you continue to heal. However, I don't know if we need to Skype so often."

"Don't you even care how we're doing?" his mother asked. "August, you didn't even ask about the mission."

"The boy has made his decision. Goodbye, August," his father said.

The connection ended.

Diane threw her arms around him. "Oh, August. I'm so sorry."

He hugged her tight, realizing once again that the Lord had given him this couple. He wasn't sure what he'd done to deserve them, but perhaps that was the point. The Lord's grace was always undeserved. "I love you both," he whispered.

When Diane moved away, Gideon wrapped an arm around him. "You're a good man, August. Don't you ever forget it."

"I won't." Standing up, he said, "I'm going to leave for a spell. I need to see Betsy."

Diane smiled. "Take your time, dear. We'll hold down the fort."

"Danke." As he walked away, August smiled, thinking that he might be a while, at that. After all, he had a very important question to ask her. And, if all went well, a lifetime to plan.

34

That morning, clouds had hung over the horizon. Sitting on the back porch, Betsy had watched them with interest, wondering if they were going to dissipate or increase and turn to rain. She and Brianna, Nate's girlfriend, had made tentative plans for the day. If it was sunny, Brianna was going to show Betsy some of the sights around Sarasota. If, on the other hand, it rained, they'd agreed to stay at their homes. Brianna had a quilt she was working on and Betsy had a book she'd been intending to finish for the last four days.

By ten o'clock, the clouds had thickened and the first raindrops fell. When her father relayed that the weather forecasters predicted rain to fall for much of the day, Betsy knew it was going to be a reading day.

After helping her mother with some cleaning, Betsy had gone to her room with her book. Unfortunately, after reading the same two paragraphs four times, Betsy realized that her heart wasn't in the activity. She honestly couldn't care less about what happened next.

Bored already, she turned to face the window and watched the rain fall. Boy, she was tired of her very plain, very clean room. It had no personality or charm.

Or, perhaps, what she was missing was her swim and golf lessons. Now that she'd accomplished both of those items on her list, she felt empty. It was kind of the same feeling she got after going to a big party or event. Her mother always called it "post-party depression." Betsy felt the silly play on words was rather apt. It turned out that accomplishing goals did make the plan-loving part of her feel let down.

She sat up. "What you need, Betsy, is something new on your life list. You need a new goal and something to plan." Staring at the rain, she bandied about different ideas. Roller skating? Hiking ten miles in the Hocking Hills?

She hadn't done either one, but she didn't exactly want to do them, either.

"Betsy?" her mother called out.

"Jah?" She hurried over to open the door. "Do you need something?" And yes, she was sounding pretty excited about that.

"Not exactly." Looking pensive — or maybe it was more thoughtful? — her mother closed Betsy's bedroom door. "Betsy, dear. You have a guest."

She was so pleased about the news, Betsy decided not to ask her mother why she was acting so strange. "Is it Brianna? She said she was going to quilt today, but maybe she changed her mind."

"No, not Brianna. Ah, August is here."

"He is? Oh, that's great." She stepped toward the door.

"Betsy, wait. I'm trying to tell you something. August is here . . . because he's come calling."

"In the middle of the day? Well, I guess it does make sense, it is really raining." Still anxious to see him, she blurted, "Oh no. Is August soaked to the skin? If his shirt is wet, maybe Daed could let him wear —"

Her mother laughed as she reached for her hand. "Daughter, stop! I'm trying to tell you something, but you're barely letting me get a word in edgewise."

Everything inside of her stilled. "What's wrong? Is something wrong with August?"

She shook her head. "Betsy, darling. August arrived with a bouquet of flowers and a box of chocolates." She swallowed. "And he is speaking to your father right now. I could be wrong, but I'm pretty sure he's here for a specific reason."

Little by little, her mother's words finally clicked. August had come calling. With flowers and candy. He was speaking to her father.

And her mother had come to her room to let her know.

Her eyes widened. "Mamm? Do . . . do you think this is w-what I think it is?" She was too afraid to say the words.

"I think it is." Studying Betsy's face, her mother tilted her head to one side. "What do you think about that?"

"I . . . I don't know." She thought about it another moment. "Maybe I'm s-surprised? Surprised, in a good way?"

"That's all I needed to know." Her mother clasped her hands together. "All right, then. I . . . well, I just wanted to come in to prepare you. In case . . . oh, never mind." She shook her head. "I don't know what I thought. You'd best go see August. He's likely a nervous wreck by now."

Betsy ran her hands down the sides of her skirt. She had on her yellow dress. It was one of her favorites, but it was probably wrinkled after lying on the bed for the last hour. Did one dress up for moments like this? Maybe, at the very least, put on a fresh dress? "Do I look all right? Do you think I should change?"

"You look fine, dear. I don't think August would want you to change a thing."

With her mother's words ringing in her ears, Betsy followed her mother out the door, then spied August sitting in the living room. On the coffee table was a bouquet of pink roses wrapped in soggy tissue paper. Next to them was a box of chocolates. Her father was nowhere to be found.

"Hi, August."

He jumped to his feet. "Betsy. Hello."

She stared at him, noticing everything about him. His blue short-sleeved shirt that was a little damp. His blond hair and dark tan and perfect features.

The way he was staring at her like she was the only thing in the entire room.

"Well, now. I think I'm going to find your father," Mamm blurted. "Maybe he's in the bedroom? I'll go check." She hurried out of the room.

Glad they were alone, Betsy walked toward the couch. "Hiya, August," she said. "I . . . I'm sorry you had to wait for me."

He jumped to his feet. "It was no problem. I needed to speak to your father anyway."

She noticed he didn't have anything to drink. "W-would you like something to drink? L-lemonade or maybe t-tea?"

"Nee." His expression eased. "Please, don't be nervous. Come sit down."

Betsy hesitated. There was a spot next to him on the couch. Or she could take the chair to his left. Which one?

He patted the spot next to him. "Sit here, Bets."

She sat down. "I see you have flowers."

"Jah. I brought you roses and chocolate." Looking doubtful, he added, "Betsy, I know a lot of things about you. I know about your life list and your golf swing. I know you're not a big fan of swimming under water and that you always need to have an inhaler nearby. But when I was at the florist, I realized that I don't know what your favorite flowers are. Or if you even like chocolate." He frowned. "Do you like chocolate?"

"I do . . . and I think my favorite flowers are pink roses."

August smiled. "That's why I fell in love with you, Betsy. You're such a kind woman, and you always say the right thing. You have a way about you that I've loved from the beginning."

Her heart felt so full as she gazed into his eyes. For most of her life, she'd wished she was different. She'd wished her body was healthier. She'd wished she could talk normally. She'd wished she wasn't so tentative around most people.

And then she met August. He'd encouraged everything she wanted to do and never seemed to care about the things she couldn't. He accepted her for who she was. He loved her.

"You make me happy, August. I love you too."

Releasing a sigh, he got down on one knee. "Betsy, I have a feeling that I should be promising all sorts of things at this moment, but all I can seem to say is that I love you and I want you to be my wife. Will you marry me?"

"Yes." She smiled. Maybe she, too, should be spouting off lots of words and promises . . . but everything else seemed superfluous.

August got to his feet, pulled her into his arms, and kissed her. Then kissed her again. Being in his arms felt perfect. Wonderful. Lovely. It was the only place she wanted to be.

35

One Year Later

The house was painted a pale yellow and had a black door. There was a profusion of freshly planted flowers in pots decorating the front porch and along the walkway. The lawn was a brilliant green and there was not one but three palm trees in a little clump in the front yard. The back of the house was even more spectacular. It had a small green lawn, but just beyond the fence was an expanse of open space. And just beyond that was the ocean.

Betsy was sure it was one of the prettiest cottages on Siesta Key with one of the best views too. She still felt like pinching herself because she got to live in it.

Sitting next to her husband on the white wicker couch on the back porch, she sighed. "Sometimes I hate to see the sun go down. Everything here is just too pretty to hide in the dark."

August chuckled as he curved an arm around her shoulders and cuddled her closer. "You say that every night."

"If I do, it's because it's still true. I still can't believe we get to enjoy these views every evening. It's a blessing."

"It is, but we're going to get to enjoy this view for years and years." His eyes lit up as he teased her. "You know, Betsy, most people like to go away from their home on their honeymoon. I was fully prepared to take you to the mountains or to Ashland or even to another part of Florida."

"I know, and I appreciate it. I just don't think any other place can hold a candle to here."

Looking out at the sun setting in the ocean, with its rays fanning out onto the current with long, broad strokes, August nodded.

"You might have a point. Siesta Key is beautiful and our haus is perfect."

"I'm glad you agree."

Betsy still couldn't believe how they'd ended up being able to get this house in the first place. The Lord really was so good. Soon after they'd gotten engaged, August's Uncle Gideon's brother passed away. That was very sad, but since he hadn't had children, he'd willed his beach cottage to

Gideon and Diane. They'd looked at the cottage, thought it was adorable but of no use to them. However, it was lovely and perfect for August and Betsy. They'd given it to them as a wedding present.

At first August had tried to refuse. The gift was too great, and housing prices on the beach could be astronomical. He'd even tried to convince his aunt and uncle to sell the house and pocket the money.

But they had refused. Gideon had even gone so far as to chide his nephew, saying that August should have better manners than to try to return a gift.

Ultimately deciding that it might be better to live in the cottage than on the golf course anyway, August had taken her here one evening. They'd sat in this very same spot, and Betsy had fallen in love.

Which was one of the reasons she'd asked that they honeymoon at home.

When the doorbell rang, August grunted. "I guess the second reason you didn't want to go away for our honeymoon has arrived."

Betsy felt like rolling her eyes. August sometimes liked to complain about all of her friends, but he ended up having as good of a time with everyone as she did.

"Don't worry, August. I'll try to keep the chatter to a minimum."

He shook his head. "Hush, frau. You know I'm only joking. Stay here and enjoy the sunset. I'll let everyone in."

August Troyer was the perfect husband for her. She was so blessed to have found him. Unable to help herself, Betsy kissed him. "Thank you."

"Anything for you, Bets." He walked inside.

The screen door leading into the kitchen allowed her to hear him open the door. And then hear the rumpus that broke out as everyone told August congratulations and teased him about having guests over so soon after their honeymoon.

"What could I do?" he said. "It was what Betsy wanted. And yes, she's out back. Go on out."

As expected, the girls hurried out while the men stayed inside and talked. Betsy had a feeling August wasn't too upset to have a moment to commiserate with the other men about the things husbands had to put up with.

When the screen door opened, she got to her feet. And there was Mary Margaret, Esther, Lilly, and Brianna. "I'm so glad you girls came over!"

"I am too," Esther said. "Michael, of course, thought you were mistaken. He said no couple was going to want company so soon, but I promised him I wasn't wrong."

"Did you have to have the same conversation, Mary?" Betsy asked.

She giggled. "Of course not. Jayson knows that I would've had all of you with me on my honeymoon if I could."

"August really didn't mind. He understands how I feel about my fellow wallflowers. Uh, no offense, Brianna."

"None taken. Honestly, I felt like a bit of a wallflower too. Until Nate made his move."

"And now the two of you are married."

She beamed. "Of course, we're not living fancy like the two of you. We're living in the small apartment in the back of Nate's family's house." She shrugged. "It's not so bad, though."

"Michael and I are still in our apartment," Esther said. "We like it too."

"Now all we have to do is find a man for you, Lilly," Mary said. "Of course, he's going to have to want to live in Pinecraft."

"I don't know how that's going to be possible," Lilly said. "I don't live here, you know."

"Why can't you?" Esther asked.

They all turned to Esther in surprise. Usually she was the one who held her tongue.

But Betsy had to agree, her question was right on target.

"What do you mean? I don't have any money saved up and it's not like my parents are going to pay for me to live here on my own."

"Then come stay with us," Betsy said.

"Sorry, but no. I'm not going to do that to you and August."

"Then stay with me," Mary said.

"You have a baby."

"Then stay with us," Esther said. "Michael is busy and I'm at the Marigold Inn a lot." She snapped her fingers. "We need another maid there. Hilda just quit. If you don't mind cleaning, I'm sure Nancy would hire you on."

"I could also ask my parents if they'd let you stay with them," Brianna said. "They're always talking about how it's too quiet now that I'm gone. I don't think they'd charge you anything."

"I couldn't stay with them."

"Not even for two weeks, until you got your first paycheck?"

Betsy smiled. "Lilly, you could move around. Stay with each of us for a week or two."

Mary nodded. "That's perfect. When you're with me, you could help me take care of Tricia."

Brianna smiled. "We've now found you places to live and a job. That is, if that's something you want to do."

Lilly bit her lip. "I don't mind cleaning, but relocating can't be easy . . ."

Thinking about everything that she'd gone through since she'd first decided to visit Mary and work on her life list, Betsy murmured, "I'm sure it won't be easy, Lilly. It's going to be hard leaving your family, moving from house to house, and starting a new job. Or it might just be hard learning to think about who you are, instead of everything everyone else assumes you to be. B-but if I can learn to swim and play golf, you can too."

"Those weren't even the toughest things Betsy had to go through," Mary pointed out. "We can't forget that she got really sick and was hospitalized for days."

"I also had to learn to stand up to my well-meaning but overprotective parents," Betsy added.

"All while falling in love with her golf instructor," Brianna finished.

Betsy could practically see the wheels turning in Lilly's head as she stared at each of the other four women, one by one.

Then she took a fortifying sip of soda.

"Being happy here in Pinecraft wasn't easy for any of you, was it?" Lilly asked.

All four of them shook their heads.

"Nate and I are both from here, but it wasn't easy for us either. We had to wait for the right time," Brianna said.

"It might not have been easy, but it wasn't impossible," Esther said. "Michael is younger than me. Neither of us are starting out with much money, either. But we still managed to make our dreams come true."

Still looking hesitant, Lilly added, "I was abandoned as a baby and went into the foster system and then was finally adopted when I was five. Some people . . ." Her voice drifted off. "Some men don't want a woman like me."

Mary looked genuinely perplexed. "I'm sorry, but like what?"

"A woman who doesn't have blood relatives. You know. A woman who doesn't have long roots."

"You know, I just thought of this, but that's the thing about lily pads, Lilly," Betsy said. "They don't need long roots to flourish and bloom. All they need is a good little pond where someone allows them to thrive. I think you could have that here."

"I'm going to do it," Lilly said. "I'm going to move to Pinecraft and learn to bloom."

Feeling her heart swell, Betsy grinned. "If that happens, it will make me so happy."

"I just hope it's possible for me to be happy here, like you all have been."

"Oh, it's possible," Betsy said. "I've decided that almost anything is possible here in Pinecraft."

Lilly laughed. "You sound so certain!"

Exchanging glances with the other women, Betsy smiled. "Of course I am. I don't know if you've heard, but Pinecraft is a pretty special place."

ABOUT THE AUTHOR

Shelley Shepard Gray is the *New York Times* and *USA Today* bestselling author of more than 100 books. Two-time winner of the HOLT Medallion and a Carol Award finalist, Gray lives in northern Ohio, where she writes full-time, bakes too much, and can often be found walking her dachshunds on her town's bike trail.